JACQUES AND HIS MASTER

MILAN KUNDERA

JACQUES AND HIS MASTER

A PLAY

Translated from the French by Simon Callow

HARPER PERENNIAL

NEW YORK • LONDON • TORONTO • SYDNEY • NEW DELHI • AUCKLAND

HARPER  PERENNIAL

First published in 1981 by Editions Gallimard as
Jacques et son maître.

First published in English in 1985 by Harper and Row,
Publishers, Inc., New York.

This translation first published in 1986 by
Faber and Faber Limited, London.

HarperCollins books may be purchased for educational,
business, or sales promotional use. For information, please e-mail
the Special Markets Department at SPsales@harpercollins.com.

First Harper Perennial edition published 2013.

Library of Congress Cataloging-in-Publication Data
is available upon request.

ISBN 978-0-06-2219077

23 24 25 26 27 LBC 9 8 7 6 5

CONTENTS

INTRODUCTION TO A VARIATION

I

When, in 1968, the Russians occupied my little country, I lost, at a stroke, any possible means of earning a living. Many people wanted to help me: one day, a theatre director came to see me to suggest that I write, under his name, an adaptation of Dostoevsky's *The Idiot*.

I therefore re-read *The Idiot* and I saw that even if I was to die of hunger, I couldn't do the job. This world of excessive gestures, of obscure profundities and of aggressive sentimentality repelled me. Suddenly, inexplicably, I felt a burst of nostalgia for *Jacques le Fataliste*.

'Wouldn't you prefer a Diderot to a Dostoevsky?'

He didn't prefer; but I couldn't rid myself of the curious notion, so in order to spend as long a time as I could in the company of Jacques and his master, I began to imagine them as characters in a play of my own.

2

Why this sudden aversion to Dostoevsky?

The anti-Russian reflex of a Czech traumatized by his country's invasion? No, because I never stopped loving Chekhov. Doubts about the aesthetic value of his work? No, because my aversion, which had taken me by surprise, had no pretensions to any objectivity.

What annoyed me about Dostoevsky was the *climate* of his books: that world where everything becomes feeling; put another way: where feeling is elevated to the level of value and of truth.

It was the third day of the Occupation. I was in my car between Prague and Budejovice (the town where Camus set *Cross Purposes*). On the roads, in the fields, in the forests, everywhere, foot-soldiers were camping. My car was stopped. Three soldiers started searching it. At the end of the operation, the officer who had ordered it asked me in Russian: '*Kak chuvstvuetes?*' which means 'How do you feel? What are your feelings?' The question was neither unkind nor ironic. On the contrary: the officer continued 'All this is a big misunderstanding. But it will sort itself out. You'll see that we love Czechs. We love you!'

The landscape devastated by thousands of tanks; the future of the country compromised for centuries; Czech statesmen arrested and taken away; and an officer of the occupying army makes you a declaration of love. Understand clearly: he didn't wish to express disagreement with the invasion; far from it. They were speaking, more or less, just like him: their attitude was based, not on the sadistic pleasure of the rapist, but on another archetype: wounded love. Why don't these Czechs (whom we love so much!) want to live with us, and like us? How sad we have to use tanks to teach them what love is!

3

Feelings are indispensable to man, but they become terrible the moment they see themselves as values, as criteria of truth, as justifications for behaviour. The noblest national sentiments are used to justfy the worst horrors; and, breast swollen with lyrical feelings, man commits the foulest acts in the sacred name of love.

When feelings replace rational thought they become the very foundation of non-understanding and intolerance; they become, as Jung says, 'the superstructure of brutality'.

The elevation of sentiment to the level of value goes back a long way, perhaps to the moment when Christianity separated from Judaism. 'Love God and do as you like' said St Augustine. The famous phrase is revealing: the criterion of truth is removed thus from the exterior to the interior: into the arbitrary realm of the subjective. A vague feeling of love ('Love God' – the Christian imperative) replaces the clarity of law (the imperative of Judaism) and becomes the criterion (oh, how blurred) of morality.

The history of Christian society is a thousand year school of feelings: Christ on the cross teaches us to worship suffering; knightly poetry discovered love; the bourgeois family makes us feel a longing for the hearth; political demagogy has succeeded in sentimentalizing the will to power. This whole long story has shaped the richness, the strength and the beauty of our feelings.

But from the Renaissance, Western sensibility has been balanced by a complementary spirit: that of reason and of doubt, of play, and of the relativity of human things. Thus the West came to its full self. When the heavy Russian irrationality fell on my country, I felt an instinctive need to breathe deeply of that spirit. And it seemed to me that nowhere was it to be found more densely concentrated than in that banquet of intelligence, humour and fantasy, *Jacques le Fataliste*.

4

If I had to define myself, I'd say that I was a hedonist trapped in a world politicized to extremes. That's the situation described in my *Laughable Loves*, which I love more than all my other books because it reflects the happiest period of my life. Curious coincidence: I finished the last of these stories (I wrote them at the thin edge of the sixties) three days before the Russians arrived.

When the French edition of the book appeared, in 1970, it was spoken of as belonging to the tradition of the century of the *Lumières*. Moved by the comparison, I then repeated, with slightly childish eagerness, how much I loved the eighteenth century. In fact, I don't particularly like the eighteenth century, I like Diderot. To be frank: I like Diderot's novels. To be absolutely precise, I like *Jacques le Fataliste*.

This vision of Diderot's work is certainly far too personal, but perhaps not altogether unjustified: it is, in fact, possible to bypass Diderot the playwright; it is possible, strictly speaking, to understand the history of philosophy without knowing the great encyclopaedist's essays; but I insist: the history of the novel would be ununderstood and incomplete without *Jacques le Fataliste*. I would go so far as to say that the book suffers from being considered exclusively in the context of the Diderot *oeuvre*, rather than in that of the novel worldwide; its real greatness can only be seen when it's put side by side with *Don Quixote*, *Tom Jones*, *Ulysses* or *Ferdydurke*.

But by comparison with Diderot's other activities, wasn't *Jacques le Fataliste* merely an entertainment? And wasn't he strongly influenced by his great model, *Tristram Shandy*?

5

I often hear it said that the novel has exhausted all its possibilities. I have the contrary impression: during the four hundred years of its history, the novel has *missed* many of the possibilities; it has left opportunities unexploited, roads unexplored and calls unheard.

Tristram Shandy by Laurence Sterne is one of these great lost directions. The history of the novel has exploited to its very limits the example of Samuel Richardson, who, in the form of the correspondence-novel, discovered the psychological possibilities of the novelist's art. It has, in compensation, paid scant attention to the perspective contained in Sterne's enterprise.

Tristram Shandy is the novel-as-game. Sterne dwells lengthily on the conception and birth of his hero, only to drop him shamelessly and more or less for good the moment he's born: he chats with his reader and loses himself in unending digressions; he starts relating an episode without ever finishing it; he inserts the dedication and the preface in the middle of the book; etc., etc., etc.

In short: Sterne does not fashion his tale according to unity of action, a principle deemed inherent in the very idea of the novel. The novel, that wonderful game with made-up characters, means for him unlimited freedom of formal invention.

An American critic, trying to defend Laurence Sterne, writes 'Tristram Shandy, although it is a comedy, is a serious work, and it is serious throughout.' God almighty, would someone please explain to me what a serious comedy is, and what is one that isn't? The sentence I quoted is devoid of sense, but it betrays to perfection the panic that seizes literary criticism in the face of anything that doesn't seem serious.

I wish to make a categorical statement: no novel worthy of the name takes the world seriously. But what does 'taking the world seriously' actually mean? What it most definitely does mean is: believing what the world wants us to believe. From *Don Quixote* to *Ulysses* the novel challenges what the world wants us to believe.

It could be objected that a novel can refuse to believe what the world wants us to believe while at the same time keeping faith with its own truth; it can refuse to take the world seriously, but still be serious itself.

But what is this 'being serious'? Serious is what someone is who believes what he makes others believe.

This is really *not* the case with *Tristram Shandy*; the book, to allude once more to the American critic, is non-serious *through-out*; it doesn't make us believe in anything: neither in the truth of the characters, the truth of the author, nor the truth of the novel as a literary genre: *everything* is put in question, *everything* is put in doubt, *everything* is a game, *everything* is entertainment (with no shame at being entertaining) and all of this with *all* the consequences implied for the form of the novel.

Yes: just like *Jacques le Fataliste*, *Tristram Shandy* is intended, in the most deliberate possible sense, to be an *entertainment*. Which is precisely how the novel was born at the dawn of the Modern Age. Its wisdom and its beauty are essentially connected to its ludic origins. Sterne rediscovered in them immense possibilities which could be used to open up new paths in the development of the novel. But nobody heard his *invitation au voyage*. No one followed him. No one – except Diderot.

He alone was responsive to this invitation to new paths. It would be absurd on this account to devalue his originality. No one denies the originality of Rousseau, Goethe or Laclos because they owed (they and the whole development of the novel) so much to the example of naïve old Richardson. If the similarity between Sterne and Diderot remains so striking, it's because their common enterprise has remained completely isolated in the history of the novel.

6

The differences between *Tristram Shandy* and *Jacques le Fataliste* are, in fact, quite as important as the similarities.

To start with, there is a *difference of temperament*: Sterne is slow; his method is deceleration; his optic is the microscope (he can stop time and isolate a single second of life the way Joyce later does).

Diderot, on the other hand, is swift; his method is acceleration; his optic is the telescope (I know of no more fascinating beginning to a novel than that of *Jacques le Fataliste*: the virtuoso change of registers; the sense of rhythm; the prestissimo of the first sentences).

Next there is a *difference of structure*: *Tristram Shandy* is a monologue by a single narrator, Tristram himself. Sterne minutely follows all the caprices of his bizarre mind.

In Diderot, five narrators, interrupting each other, tell the stories in the novel: the author himself (in conversation with his reader); the Master (in conversation with Jacques); Jacques (in conversation with his master); the innkeeper (in conversation with her audience); and the Marquis des Arcis. The basic method of each individual story is dialogue (of unequalled virtuosity). But the narrators recount these dialogues within dialogues (the dialogues are encased in dialogue) in such a way that the whole novel is nothing but a vast, very loud, conversation.

Again, there is a *difference of spirit*: the Reverend Sterne's book is a compromise between the freethinking spirit and the sentimental spirit, a nostalgic memory of Rabelaisian gaiety in the prudish antechamber of the Victorian Age.

Diderot's novel is an explosion of impertinent unselfcensoring freedom and eroticism unjustified by sentimental excuses.

Finally, there is a *difference in the degree of realistic illusion*: Sterne stands chronology on its head, but the events of the novel are firmly anchored in time and place. The characters are bizarre, but equipped with everything that we need to be able to believe in their real existence.

Diderot creates a space never before glimpsed in the history of the novel: a stage without scenery: where do they come from? We don't know. What are their names? None of our business. How old are they? No, Diderot does nothing to make us believe that the characters really exist at a specified moment in time. In the entire world-wide history of the novel, *Jacques le Fataliste* is the most radical rejection of both the illusion of realism and the aesthetic of the so-called psychological novel.

7

The method of the *Reader's Digest* faithfully reflects the deepest tendencies of our times and makes me think that one day the whole of our cultural heritage will be completely rewritten and completely forgotten underneath its rewriting. Movie versions and stage versions of great novels are nothing more than a kind of *Reader's Digest*.

It's not a question of defending the untouchable virginity of works of art. Obviously, Shakespeare, as much as anyone, rewrote other people's work. But he didn't adapt them; he used a work as a theme to make his own variation, of which he was sovereign author. Diderot borrowed from Sterne the whole story of Jacques wounded in the knee, transported by cart and looked after by a beautiful woman. That done, he neither imitated nor adapted. He wrote a variation on Sterne's theme.

On the other hand, movie and theatre transpositions of *Anna Karenina* are adaptations: that is, reductions. The more the adapter attempts to conceal himself discreetly behind the novel, the more he betrays it. By reducing it he deprives it not only of charm but also of sense.

To stay with Tolstoy: in a way radically new in the history of the novel, he posed the question of human action: he discovered the fatal importance in a decision of causes impossible to grasp rationally. Why did Anna kill herself? Tolstoy goes so far as to use an almost Joycean interior monologue to demonstrate the tissue of irrational motivations which guide his heroine. Every adaptation of this novel, inevitably, by the very nature of the *Reader's Digest*, tries to make the causes of Anna's behaviour clear and logical, to rationalize them; the adaptation thus becomes quite simply the negation of the novel's originality.

The reverse is also true: if the sense of a novel survives rewriting, that indirectly proves its mediocrity. In world literature, there are two novels which are absolutely irreducible, totally unrewriteable: *Tristram Shandy* and *Jacques le Fataliste*. How can their masterly disorder be simplified in such a way that something remains? And what should remain?

It is possible, of course, to detach the story of Mme de La Pommeraye and make a play or a film out of it (it's been done). But all that is left is a banal anecdote stripped of all its charm. In fact, the beauty of the story is inseparable from the way in which Diderot tells it: i) a working-class women recounts events which occur in a milieu to which she is a complete stranger; ii) any melodramatic identification with the characters is impossible, given that the telling is constantly and incongruously interrupted with other stories and speeches and also iii) incessantly commented on, analysed, discussed but iv) each commentator draws a different conclusion, the story of Mme de La Pommeraye being an *antimorality*.

Why do I allow this to exercise me so much? Because I wish to cry, with Jacques and his master, 'Death to those who rewrite what has already been written! May their balls and their ears be cut off!'

And, naturally, to state that *Jacques and his Master* is not an adaptation; it's my own play, my own 'variation on Diderot', or rather, since it was conceived in admiration, my Homage to Diderot.

This 'variation-homage' is a multiple meeting: between the writers, but also between the centuries. And between the novel and the theatre. The form of a dramatic piece has always been much more rigid and rule-bound than that of the novel. The theatre has never had its Laurence Sterne. I have written not merely a Homage to Diderot, but also a Homage to the Novel, trying to lend my comedy the formal liberty that Diderot-the-novelist found, but which Diderot-the-theatre-writer never knew.

The construction is this: on the fragile structure of Jacques's voyage with his master are based three love stories: the master's; Jacques's; and Mme de La Pommeraye's. While the first two are lightly linked (the second one very lightly) to the outcome of the voyage, the third, which occupies the whole of the second act, is, from the technical point of view, an episode, pure and simple (it has no integral connection with the main action). It's an obvious flouting of what are known as the laws of dramatic construction. But that's precisely where I saw my opportunity: to renounce strict unity of action and create coherence of the whole by more subtle means: by the technique of polyphony (the three stories are not told one after another, but intermingled) and by the technique of variations (each story is in fact the variation of the others). Thus this play which is a 'variation on Diderot' is at the same time a 'homage to variation form', just as was, seven years later, my novel, *The Book of Laughter and Forgetting*.

For a Czech author in the seventies, it was strange to think that *Jacques le Fataliste* (also written in the seventies!) was never printed during its author's life and that only manuscript copies could be distributed to a limited and confidential public. What in Diderot's time was an exception has become, two hundred years later in Prague, the common lot of all important Czech writers who, barred from the printing presses, can only see their work in typescript. This started with the Russian invasion, it continues, and there is every likelihood that it will continue.

I wrote *Jacques and his Master* for my private pleasure and perhaps with the vague notion that one day it might be allowed to play in a Czech theatre under an assumed name. As a signature, I spread through the text (another game, another variation!) memories of my earlier work: the Jacques and his master evoke the couple from *The Golden Apple of Eternal Desire* (*Laughable Loves*): a few phrases are quotations from my farce (*Ptakovina*) put on in Prague in 1968 and 1969 and then banned; there's an allusion to *Life is Elsewhere* and another to *The Farewell Party*. Yes, they were memories; the whole play was a farewell to my life as a writer, 'farewell in the form of an entertainment'. *The Farewell Party*, which I completed at more or less the same time, was to have been my last novel. However, I lived through this time without having the bitter taste of personal defeat, because of the degree to which the private farewell was part of another, huge one, which concerned me.

Faced with the eternity of the Russian night, in Prague I lived out the violent end of modern culture as it has been conceived at the dawn of the Modern Age, founded on the individual and his reason, on pluralism of thought and on tolerance. In a tiny Western country, I lived out the end of the West. That was it, the big farewell.

With an illiterate peasant as his servant, Don Quixote left his house one day to do battle with his enemies. One hundred and fifty years later, Toby Shandy made his garden into a large model of a battlefield; there, he gave himself over to memories of his soldierly youth, faithfully assisted by his valet Trim. He limped, just like Jacques who, ten years later, entertained his master during his voyage. He was as chatty and opinionated as, a hundred and fifty years later in the Austro–Hungarian army, the orderly Josef Švetjk, who so amused and horrified his master, Lieutenant Lukac. Thirty years later, waiting for Godot, Vladimir and his servant already find themselves alone on the empty stage of the world. The voyage is at an end.

The valet and his master have crossed the whole of modern Western history. In Prague, city of the big farewell, I heard their dwindling laughter. With love and anguish, I held on to that laughter the way one holds on to fragile and perishable things which are doomed.

Paris, July 1981

JACQUES AND HIS MASTER

I imagine Jacques as a man of at least 40. He is the same age as
his master or older. François Germond, director of the excellent
Geneva Production, had a most interesting idea: when Jacques
and his master meet up again in scene six of Act Three, they are
already old, years having passed since the previous scene.

DESIGN: Throughout the play, the stage never changes; it's
divided into two parts: one part, at the front, lower, and the
other, behind, which is elevated to a large rostrum. All the
action which takes place in the present is played on the
forestage; the scenes from the past are staged on the area
behind.

Right at the back of the stage (and therefore on the elevated
rostrum) there is a staircase, or a ladder, leading to a closet.

Most of the time, the stage (which must be as abstract and
simple as it can possibly be) is entirely empty. Only for certain
episodes do the actors themselves bring on tables, chairs, etc. It
is important to guard against ornamental, illustrative or
symbolic elements in the design. They go against the spirit of
the play.

The action takes place in the eighteenth century, but the
eighteenth century as we imagine it today. Just as the play's
language is not a reconstruction of the language of another time,
nor should the historical character of the set or the costumes be
insisted on. The historical authenticity of the characters
(particularly the two central ones) though undeniable, should be
slightly toned down.

CHARACTERS

JACQUES
JACQUES'S MASTER
INNKEEPER
CHEVALIER DE SAINT-OUEN
YOUNG BIGRE
OLD BIGRE
JUSTINE
MARQUIS
MOTHER
DAUGHTER
AGATHE
AGATHE'S MOTHER
AGATHE'S FATHER
POLICE OFFICER
BAILIFF

ACT ONE

SCENE ONE

JACQUES *and his* MASTER *come on stage. They take several steps, and* JACQUES's *eyes fall on the audience;* JACQUES *stops . . .*

JACQUES: (*Confidentially*) Sir . . . (*Pointing out the audience to his* MASTER) What they up to, looking at us like that?

HIS MASTER: (*Giving a start and adjusting his clothing, as if he were frightened of attracting attention by sloppy dressing*) Behave as if no one were there.

JACQUES: (*To the audience*) Wouldn't you rather look somewhere else? What do you want to know? Where we came from?
(*Waves behind him with his arm.*) Back there. And where we're going? (*With philosophical weight*) Who knows where they're going, eh? (*To the audience*) Do you know, any of you, where you're going?

MASTER: Jacques, I'm frightened of knowing where we're going.

JACQUES: Frightened?

MASTER: (*Sadly*) Yes. But I have no intention whatever of letting you into my melancholy duties.

JACQUES: Believe me, sir, no one ever knows where he's going. But, as my old captain always used to say: it's all written up there.

MASTER: He was right . . .

JACQUES: The devil poke Justine and the lousy storehouse where I first lost my cherry!

MASTER: Why are you insulting a woman, Jacques?

JACQUES: Because, after I lost my cherry, I got pissed. My old man, really narked, bashed me over the head. A regiment was passing by, I signed up, a war broke out, and I got a bullet in me knee. Which then led to a whole load of adventures. If it hadn't been for that bullet, for example, I don't think I'd ever have fallen in love.

MASTER: You've been in love? You never told me.

JACQUES: There's a lot of things I've never told you.

MASTER: Come along then: tell me how you fell in love. Let's have the story.

JACQUES: Where was I? Oh yes, the bullet in me knee. I was piled up under a load of dead and wounded. They found me next morning and flung me on a cart – destination the hospital. It was a terrible road and I screamed with pain at every bump. Suddenly we stopped. I ask to get out. It was at the edge of a village and in front of the door of this shack was a young woman.

MASTER: Ah. I'm with you now.

JACQUES: She goes back inside: comes out with a bottle and gives me some to drink. They wanted me to get back into the cart, but I grabbed hold of her dress. Then I passed out and when I came round again, I was in the shade with her husband and kids all around, while she made compresses for me.

MASTER: You rat! I know what you're going to say next.

JACQUES: You don't know anything of the sort.

MASTER: This man takes you into his house, and this is how you thank him.

JACQUES: Sir. Are we masters of our actions? My old captain always used to say: everything that happens to us down here, good and bad, is written up above. You know any way, dear Master, to wipe out what is written? Can I not be? Can I be someone else? If I'm me, can I do anything but what I do?

MASTER: One thing puzzles me, though: are you a rat because it was written up above? Or is it written up above because they knew you would be a rat? Which is cause and which effect?

JACQUES: Dunno, sir, but kindly refrain from calling me a rat.

MASTER: A man who cuckolds his benefactor.

JACQUES: He was *not* my benefactor. You should have seen how he treated his wife because she took pity on me.

MASTER: He was absolutely right... Jacques, what was she like? Describe her.

JACQUES: The young woman?

MASTER: Yes.

JACQUES: (*After a moment's hesitation*) Medium height...

MASTER: (*Not very pleased*) Hum.

JACQUES: But on the large side.

MASTER: (*With an approving nod of his head*) On the large side.

JACQUES: Yes.

MASTER: I do like that.

JACQUES: (*With an expressive movement of his hands*) Lovely breasts.

MASTER: Bigger bum than breasts?

JACQUES: (*Hesitating*) No. Breasts bigger.

MASTER: (*Sadly*) Shame.

JACQUES: You like big bums?

MASTER: Yes ... like Agathe's ... The eyes. How were they?

JACQUES: Her eyes? Don't remember. But her hair was black.

MASTER: Agathe was blonde.

JACQUES: There's nothing I can do about it, sir, if she wasn't like your Agathe. You have to take her as she is. But she did have long, pretty legs.

MASTER: (*Dreaming*) Long legs! You give me great pleasure!

JACQUES: And a really majestic bum.

MASTER: Majestic! Seriously?

JACQUES: (*Demonstrating*) Like this.

MASTER: Oh you rat. The more you talk the angrier I get. Your benefactor's wife! You actually –

JACQUES: No, sir. Nothing at all happened between this woman and me.

MASTER: Why are you telling me, then? Why are we wasting our time on her?

JACQUES: You keep interrupting me, sir. It's a very bad habit.

MASTER: I already have a deep longing for her.

JACQUES: I tell you I'm in bed, with a bullet in me knee, that I'm suffering the agony of the martyrs – and all you think about is pleasure. Plus you keep adding in Agathe.

MASTER: Don't you dare utter her name.

JACQUES: You were the one who uttered it.

MASTER: Have you had the experience of madly desiring a woman who wasn't interested at all? At all?

JACQUES: Yes. Justine.

MASTER: Justine? The one you lost your cherry with?

JACQUES: Exactly.

MASTER: Tell.

JACQUES: After you, sir. You're the Master.

SCENE TWO

At the back, on the rostrum, other characters have been appearing.
YOUNG BIGRE is seated on the steps, JUSTINE stands above him.
Another couple are on the opposite side of the stage. AGATHE is
sitting on a chair brought for her by the CHEVALIER DE SAINT-
OUEN who stands by her side.

SAINT-OUEN: (*Calling the MASTER*) Hullo! My friend!

JACQUES: (*He turns at the same time as his MASTER and nods in the direction of AGATHE.*) That's her? (*The MASTER agrees.*) And the man next to her?

MASTER: A friend, Saint-Ouen. He introduced us. (*Indicating JUSTINE with a glance*) The other one over there, that yours?

JACQUES: Yes, but I prefer yours.

MASTER: And I yours. More flesh. You wouldn't like to swap?

JACQUES: We should have thought of that at the time. 'S too late now.

MASTER: (*Sighing*) Yes. Too late. And who's the young blood next to her?

JACQUES: Bigre, a chum. We both wanted that girl, both of us. But for impenetrable reasons, he got her and I didn't.

MASTER: Me too.

SAINT-OUEN: (*Who has approached the* MASTER *up to the edge of the rostrum*) My friend, you haven't been very discreet. The parents are worried for their little girl's reputation.

MASTER: (*To* JACQUES, *outraged*) Dirty bourgeois! Showering their daughter with presents causes them anxiety?

SAINT-OUEN: No, no, no. They have great respect for you. They simply want you to state your intentions clearly. Otherwise, you'll have to stop going there.

MASTER: (*Indignantly, to* JACQUES) When I think he took me to her house! And encouraged me! And told me how easy it would be!

SAINT-OUEN: I'm merely conveying the message I've been charged with.

MASTER: (*To* SAINT-OUEN) Fine. (*He climbs on to the rostrum.*) I charge you to convey to them that I cannot be relied upon to place the ring on her finger. And tell Agathe she should be rather more tender in future if she means to keep me. I do not propose to waste my time and money on her when I could use both more gainfully elsewhere.

(SAINT-OUEN *listens to the* MASTER's *message, and returns to near* AGATHE.)

JACQUES: Bravo, Master! That's the you I like! Courageous for once, eh?

MASTER: (*To* JACQUES, *from the rostrum*) It comes to me from time to time . . . I stopped seeing her.

SAINT-OUEN: (*Moving in an arc towards the* MASTER) I conveyed your message word for word, but I can't help feeling that you were a little cruel.

JACQUES: My master? Cruel?

SAINT-OUEN: (*To* JACQUES) Shut it, flunkey. (*To the* MASTER) The whole family is shattered by your silence. As for Agathe . . .

MASTER: Agathe?

SAINT-OUEN: Agathe cries.

MASTER: She cries.

SAINT-OUEN: All day long.

MASTER: So, Saint-Ouen, what do you think would happen if I showed up again?

SAINT-OUEN: A bad mistake, in my opinion. You can't retreat. If you went back now, you'd be lost. You have to teach these shopkeepers a lesson.

MASTER: But if they never ask me back?

SAINT-OUEN: They'll ask you back.

MASTER: But if it goes on too long?

SAINT-OUEN: D'you want to be the slave or the master?

MASTER: Yes, but she's crying . . .

SAINT-OUEN: Better she should cry than you.

MASTER: But what if they never ask me back?

SAINT-OUEN: They'll ask you back. Don't worry. You must use the situation to your advantage. Agathe must be made to see that you're not going to eat out of her hand, and that she must pull her weight . . . tell me though . . . cut your tongue out and hope to die: has anything ever gone on between you?

MASTER: No.

SAINT-OUEN: Your discretion does you credit.

MASTER: Not at all. It's the plain truth.

SAINT-OUEN: What? Not one tiny moment of weakness?

MASTER: Not one.

SAINT-OUEN: I'm afraid you may have behaved like a berk.

MASTER: But what about you, Saint-Ouen? Mm? Have you never wanted her?

SAINT-OUEN: Certainly I have. But then you arrived and I became pure spirit for Agathe. We remained good friends, but nothing more. My only one consolation is this: if my best friend sleeps with her, it will be as if I had.
(*With these words, he goes off to the back of the stage in the direction of* AGATHE, *who remains seated.*)

JACQUES: You observe, Master, how closely I listen. Not once have I interrupted you. If only you could take a leaf –

MASTER: You're boasting about not interrupting in order to interrupt.

JACQUES: If I cut you off in mid-stream, I'm only following your example.

MASTER: As a master, it is my absolute right to interrupt my servant whenever I wish. My servant, on the other hand, has no right to interrupt his master.

JACQUES: I'm not interrupting, sir, I'm talking to you, like you always said I should. And let me tell you frankly: I don't like this friend of yours. I reckon he's going to make you marry his girlfriend.

MASTER: Shut up! I'm not speaking to you any more. (*He gets off the rostrum in a huff.*)

JACQUES: Sir! No! Go on.

MASTER: Why? With your pretentious powers of prediction, in the worst possible taste, you know everything in advance.

JACQUES: You're right, sir, but do go on. Unless I'm wrong, that's the only way things can turn out, but what I can't guess is the delightful details of your dealings with Saint-Ouen and all the little caprices of the plot.

MASTER: You've worn me out. I have nothing to say.

JACQUES: Go on. Please.

MASTER: If you want to make it up, *you* must tell *your* story, while I interrupt whenever I feel like it. I want to know how you lost your cherry, and you can rest assured I shall frequently interrupt you during your first bout of love.

SCENE THREE

JACQUES: As you wish, sir. It's your right. (*Turns round, and climbs up the same ladder as* JUSTINE *and* YOUNG BIGRE. OLD BIGRE *is at the foot of the ladder.*) My godfather, old Bigre, is in his wheelwright's shop. The stepladder leads up

to the granary which is where young Bigre's bed is – young
Bigre, my friend.

OLD BIGRE: Bigre! Bigre! Bloody loafer!

JACQUES: Old man Bigre used to sleep in his shop. When he
was sound asleep, young Bigre would gently open the door
and Justine would go up the stairs into the closet.

OLD BIGRE: The Angelus has already been rung and you're still
snoring like a pig. You want me to come up there and get
you down here with my broom?

JACQUES: That night, they'd had so much pleasure together
that they just couldn't wake up.

YOUNG BIGRE: (*From the granary*) Calm down, dad!

OLD BIGRE: The farmer's coming for his axle any moment now!
Get on with it, will you!

YOUNG BIGRE: I'm here! (*Coming down the ladder buttoning up
his pants.*)

MASTER: So Justine couldn't get out?

JACQUES: Trapped.

MASTER: (*Roaring with laughter*) I imagine she was in a bit of a
tight corner!

OLD BIGRE: Ever since he went crazy for that slag, all he can do
is sleep. If only she was worth it. But that one? A tart like
that? If my poor dear dead wife had seen it, she would've
thrashed the one, and gouged the other's eyes out
after Mass on Sunday. But me – like a fool, I put up
with it, I don't know why. Well, it's all gonna change.
(*To* YOUNG BIGRE) Get that axle and take it to the
farmer.
(*Off goes* YOUNG BIGRE *with the axle over his shoulder.*)

MASTER: Justine heard all this from upstairs?

JACQUES: Too right!

OLD BIGRE: Jesus God, God Jesus, where's my pipe? Needless
to say that lump of nothing will have taken it. Better see if
it's upstairs. (*Climbs the staircase.*)

MASTER: What about Justine? What about Justine?

JACQUES: Slid under the bed.

MASTER: And young Bigre?

JACQUES: When he'd delivered his axle, he ran to my place. Look, I said to him: go for a walk round the village and I'll keep your old man busy to give Justine a chance to escape. Give me a bit of time, though. (*Climbs on to the rostrum. The* MASTER *smiles.*) Why are you smiling?

MASTER: Nothing.

OLD BIGRE: (*Coming down from the granary*) Pleased to see you, godson. What you doing up so early?

JACQUES: I'm going home.

OLD BIGRE: Oh godson, godson, you been a naughty boy?

JACQUES: Can't deny it.

OLD BIGRE: I wouldn't be surprised if you and that lad of mine weren't up to the same tricks! You spend the night out?

JACQUES: Can't deny it.

OLD BIGRE: What, whoring?

JACQUES: Yes – but with my dad, you can't even talk about it.

OLD BIGRE: Quite right, he ought to give you a good thwack round the head, and I ought to do the same to my boy. But come on, let's have some breakfast. The wine's wise, know what I mean?

JACQUES: Please. Godfather. I'm dropping.

OLD BIGRE: Didn't stint yourself, I see. Hope she was worth the effort. All right, no more chat – look, my boy's out, go upstairs, snuggle up in his bed.
(JACQUES *climbs the staircase.*)

MASTER: (*Shouting at* JACQUES) Traitor! *Rotter!* I should have guessed...

OLD BIGRE: These kids! Bloody kids!... (*Noises and stifled cries from the granary.*) He's dreaming, that one... obviously spent a very lively night.

MASTER: Dreaming! He's not dreaming at all! He's terrorizing her, that's what he's doing. She's fighting him off, but she's frightened of being found out so she has to keep quiet. You beast, you should be charged with rape.

JACQUES: (*From the granary*) I don't know whether I raped her, sir, but I do know that it was pretty good – for both of us, her and me. She just made me promise...

MASTER: What did you promise, worm?

JACQUES: That Bigre would know nothing.

MASTER: And that promise made sure things went well.

JACQUES: Better and better!

MASTER: How many times?

JACQUES: A *lot* of times, and always better and better.
    (YOUNG BIGRE *comes back*.)

OLD BIGRE: Where have you been all this time? Get hold of this
    wheel and finish it off on the doorstep.

YOUNG BIGRE: Why on the doorstep?

OLD BIGRE: So as not to wake Jacques up.

YOUNG BIGRE: Jacques?

OLD BIGRE: Yes, Jacques. He's upstairs, snoring. Who'd be a
    father? You're all the same. Well, come on, look lively,
    grown to the spot, have you?
    (YOUNG BIGRE *rushes to the staircase and is about to climb
    up*.)
    Where are you going? Let the poor kid sleep!

YOUNG BIGRE: (*Loud*) Papa! Papa!

OLD BIGRE: He's dead tired!

YOUNG BIGRE: Let me past!

OLD BIGRE: Push off! How would you like to be woken up
    when you're sleeping?

MASTER: And Justine heard all this?

JACQUES: (*Coming to the top of the stairs*) As clear as you can
    hear me!

MASTER: Oh, lovely! You first-class shit! And what did you
    do?

JACQUES: I laughed.

MASTER: You should swing for that. What about her?

JACQUES: She tore her hair out, lifted her eyes up to heaven and
    wrung her hands.

MASTER: Jacques, you are a savage and you have a heart of
    tempered steel.

JACQUES: (*Descending the stairs, very seriously*) Not true, sir. I
    have great sensibility. But I was keeping it for a better
    occasion. People who spread their sensibility here,

there and everywhere don't have any left when they need it.

OLD BIGRE: (*To* JACQUES) Ah! There you are. Sleep well? You certainly needed to. (*To his son*) Look at him! Fresh as a new born babe! Go and get a bottle from the cellar. *Now* you won't say no to a spot of breakfast.
(YOUNG BIGRE *finds a bottle and the old boy fills three glasses.*)

YOUNG BIGRE: (*Pushing his glass away*) I'm not thirsty this early in the morning.

OLD BIGRE: Not thirsty?

YOUNG BIGRE: No.

OLD BIGRE: Ah ha ha! I know what's up! (*To* JACQUES) There's a bit of Justine behind all this! Look how long he was out, he must have stopped by at Justine's and found her with someone else! I told you she was a slag. (*To* JACQUES) So he takes it out on this poor innocent bottle.

JACQUES: You may have hit the nail on the head.

YOUNG BIGRE: Jacques, we've had enough of this joke.

OLD BIGRE: Well, just because you don't want to drink, it doesn't mean we can't: (*Lifts his glass*) Your health, godson...

JACQUES: And yours... (*To* YOUNG BIGRE) Come on, chum, drink. I'm sure you're making a mountain out of a molehill.

YOUNG BIGRE: I've already said I'm not drinking.

JACQUES: You'll see her again and it'll all be all right. You have nothing to fear.

OLD BIGRE: No – let her make him suffer... meanwhile, you pack off to your dad so as he can forgive you for your escapades. Bloody kids! All the same... load of louse-infected layabouts... All right, let's go.
(*Takes* JACQUES *by the arm and leads him off.* YOUNG BIGRE *goes up the staircase. After a few steps,* JACQUES *leaves* OLD BIGRE *and turns towards his* MASTER, *while the old boy leaves the stage.*)

MASTER: That's a wonderful story. It teaches you to know women better, and to know your friends better.

(*On the rostrum,* SAINT-OUEN *starts to come slowly towards* JACQUES *and his* MASTER.)

JACQUES: You think that a friend would turn his back on your mistress if he had the opportunity?

SCENE FOUR

SAINT-OUEN: Friend! Dear friend! Come over here! (*He's at the edge of the rostrum and stretches out his arm to the* MASTER, *who's below the rostrum. The* MASTER *climbs up to the rostrum and joins* SAINT-OUEN *who takes him by the arm and promenades him up and down.*) My dear friend! It's wonderful having a friend for whom one feels really sincere friendship . . .

MASTER: I'm touched, Saint-Ouen.

SAINT-OUEN: Yes, of all friends, you, my friend, are the best of friends, whereas I, my friend . . .

MASTER: You? You too, of all my friends – you are the best of friends.

SAINT-OUEN: (*Lowering his head*) I'm afraid, my friend, you don't know me.

MASTER: I know you like I know myself!

SAINT-OUEN: If you *knew* me, you wouldn't want to know me . . .

MASTER: Don't say that.

SAINT-OUEN : I am a worthless man. No, there's no other word: worthless. That's the only way I can describe myself to you. I am a worthless man.

MASTER: I won't allow you to humble yourself before me.

SAINT-OUEN: Worthless!

MASTER: No!

SAINT-OUEN: A worthless man!

MASTER: (*Kneeling*) Be quiet, my friend. Your words rend my heart. What is it that's tormenting you? What have you done that's so terrible?

SAINT-OUEN: There's a blot on my past life. Only a blot, just the one, in fact, but ...

MASTER: There you are: just one blot. That's nothing. What is it?

SAINT-OUEN: Just one blot can blacken a whole life.

MASTER: One swallow doesn't make a summer. Just one blot is no blot at all.

SAINT-OUEN: No. No. It may be just one blot, all on its own, but that one is terrible. I, Saint-Ouen, I, yes, me, I once betrayed, I *betrayed* – a friend.

MASTER: All right. Now: how did it happen?

SAINT-OUEN: We were both, he and I, paying calls on the same young lady. He was in love with her, and she was in love with me. He was keeping her, and I reaped the benefit. I never had the courage to tell him. But I must. When I come across him again, I must tell him everything, I must make a full confession if I want to rid myself of the dreadful secret that's dragging me down ...

MASTER: That would be good, Saint-Ouen.

SAINT-OUEN: That's your advice?

MASTER: Yes, that's my advice.

SAINT-OUEN: And how do you think my friend will take it?

MASTER: He'll be touched by your frankness and penitence. He'll take you in his arms.

SAINT-OUEN: You really think so?

MASTER: I really do.

SAINT-OUEN: What about you? Would you do the same?

MASTER: Me? Of course.

SAINT-OUEN: (*Opening his arms*) My friend! Take me in your arms!

MASTER: Pardon?

SAINT-OUEN: Embrace me! The friend I deceived is you.

MASTER: (*Shattered*) Agathe?

SAINT-OUEN: Yes ... Ah! You're unhappy! – You can go back on what you said. Go on! Do what you like with me! You're right: what I did is unforgivable! Leave me! Abandon me! Hate me! ... oh if only you knew what that wretched girl

has made me do! If only you knew how I suffered, playing
a part that was forced on me!

SCENE FIVE

(*Intercut dialogue*)

YOUNG BIGRE *and* JUSTINE *come down the staircase and sit side
by side. They seem exhausted.*

JUSTINE: I swear! I swear on my mother's and my father's
head!
YOUNG BIGRE: I'll never believe you!
(JUSTINE *breaks down sobbing.*)
MASTER: (*To* SAINT-OUEN) That wretched girl! But Saint-
Ouen, how could you, how could *you* . . .
SAINT-OUEN: Don't torture me, friend!
JUSTINE: I swear he never even touched me!
YOUNG BIGRE: Liar!
MASTER: How could you!
YOUNG BIGRE: With that rat!
(JUSTINE *sobs some more.*)
SAINT-OUEN: How could I? Because I'm worthless! The most
worthless man on the face of the earth. I have as a friend
the best of men, and I have ignominiously betrayed him.
You ask me why? Because I'm a rat! That's all: just a rat!
JUSTINE: He is not a rat! He's your friend!
YOUNG BIGRE: (*Enraged*) Friend?
JUSTINE: Friend – if only you knew it. He never so much as
touched me!
YOUNG BIGRE: Shut up.
SAINT-OUEN: Yes, just a rat. That's all.
MASTER: No. Stop shitting on yourself.
SAINT-OUEN: I do! I shit on myself!
MASTER: Despite everything that's happened, you mustn't shit
on yourself.
JUSTINE: He told me that he was your friend and that he could

have nothing to do with me, even if we were alone on a
desert island.

MASTER: Stop making yourself ill.

YOUNG BIGRE: He said that?

JUSTINE: Yes!

SAINT-OUEN: I want to be ill.

MASTER: We're both victims of the same monster, you just as
much as me! She seduced you! You've been honest and told
me everything. You're still my friend.

YOUNG BIGRE: On a desert island? He said that?

JUSTINE: Yes!

SAINT-OUEN: I'm unworthy of your friendship.

MASTER: On the contrary, that's why you're worthy of it.
You've paid with the torments of remorse.

YOUNG BIGRE: He really said he was my friend and that he
wouldn't be able to touch you even if you were alone
together on a desert island?

JUSTINE: Yes!

SAINT-OUEN: You're so generous!

MASTER: Embrace me!
(*They embrace.*)

YOUNG BIGRE: He really said he wouldn't touch you even if
you were alone together on a desert island?

JUSTINE: Yes!

YOUNG BIGRE: A desert island? Swear it.

JUSTINE: I swear!

MASTER: Come on, let's have a drink.

JACQUES: Oh sir, this is really painful to watch.

MASTER: To our friendship, which no scrubber is going to kill!

YOUNG BIGRE: A desert island. I've done him an injustice, he's
a real friend.

JACQUES: It seems to me, Master, that our adventures are
strangely similar.

MASTER: (*Coming out of the action*) What?

JACQUES: I say, our adventures are strangely similar.

YOUNG BIGRE: Jacques is a true friend.

JUSTINE: Your best.

SAINT-OUEN: Just now all I can think of is revenge. That awful girl has abused us, and we must be revenged: both of us. Just tell me what I must do, and I'll do it!

MASTER: (*Annoyed by* JACQUES's *last observation, to* SAINT-OUEN) Later. We'll finish the story later . . .

SAINT-OUEN: No, no! Now! Immediately! I'll do whatever you say! Just tell me what you want.

MASTER: I will, but later. At this precise moment I want to know how things worked out for Jacques.
(MASTER *comes down from the rostrum.*)

YOUNG BIGRE: Jacques!
(JACQUES *leaps on to the rostrum and goes to* YOUNG BIGRE.)

YOUNG BIGRE: I want to thank you. You're my best friend. (*Kisses him*) And now, kiss Justine. (JACQUES *hesitates.*) Go on, now, don't be shy, you've got every right to kiss her in front of me! I command you! (JACQUES *kisses* JUSTINE.) We're the three best friends in the world, for life, till death . . . A desert island . . . is it true you wouldn't touch her, not even on a desert island?

JACQUES: A friend's woman? You crazy?

YOUNG BIGRE: You are the most faithful friend!

MASTER: You filthy pig. (JACQUES *comes back to his* MASTER.) But my adventure is still far from over.

JACQUES: Being cuckolded wasn't enough for you?

YOUNG BIGRE: (*At the very height of happiness*) The most faithful woman! The most faithful friend! I'm happy as a lord!
(*As he says the last couple of speeches* YOUNG BIGRE *leaves with* JUSTINE. SAINT-OUEN *stays to hear the first speeches of the next scene, then he goes too.*)

MASTER: My adventure ended up very badly: the worst possible ending an adventure can have . . .

JACQUES: And what is the worst ending an adventure can have?

MASTER: Think about it.

JACQUES: I will . . . what could be the worst ending an adventure . . . ? But you know, sir, my adventure is far from having come to an end. I'd lost my cherry, I'd found my best friend. I was so happy I got arseholed. My father bashed me round the head. A regiment was passing by, I sign up on an impulse, then I'm in the middle of a campaign, I get a bullet in the knee, I'm shoved on a cart, it stops in front of a shack and this woman appears on the doorstep . . .

MASTER: You already told me.

JACQUES: You going to keep chipping in?

MASTER: All right then, get on with it.

JACQUES: I won't. Not if you're going to keep interrupting.

MASTER: (*Humorously*) Fine. In that case, let's take a few steps . . . there's still quite a way to go . . . God almighty, we haven't got horses. How come?

JACQUES: You're forgetting we're on stage. How could we have horses?

MASTER: Thanks to some ridiculous play, I have to go on foot! Even though the master who invented us allotted us horses.

JACQUES: That's the danger of being invented by too many masters.

MASTER: I sometimes wonder, Jacques, whether we're good inventions. D'you think we've been well invented?

JACQUES: Which inventor are you referring to? The great one in the sky? Up there?

MASTER: It was written, up there, that someone down here would write our story. What I want to know is: is it well written? I mean, was he talented?

JACQUES: If he wasn't talented, he wouldn't have written.

MASTER: What?

JACQUES: I'm saying, if he wasn't talented, he wouldn't have written.

MASTER: (*Roaring with laughter*) You've just proved that you're only a servant after all. You think that people who write have talent? What about the young poet who one day came to see our master?

JACQUES: I don't know any poet.

MASTER: Clearly you won't know much about our master. You're just an ignorant servant.

(*The* INNKEEPER *comes on stage. She comes towards* JACQUES *and his* MASTER *and curtsies.*)

INNKEEPER: Welcome, gentlemen.

MASTER: Welcome? Where are we, Madam?

INNKEEPER: The Stag Inn.

MASTER: I've never heard that name before.

INNKEEPER: Tables! Chairs!

(*Two* WAITERS *rush on stage with tables and chairs which they put in front of* JACQUES *and his* MASTER.)

INNKEEPER: It was written that on your travels you would stop at our inn, where you would eat, drink, sleep and listen to the *patronne* who is famed for miles around on account of the incredible size of her gob.

MASTER: As if my servant weren't enough.

INNKEEPER: What is the gentlemen's favour?

MASTER: (*Gazing at the* INNKEEPER *with greed*) That needs a little thought.

INNKEEPER: It doesn't need any thought at all. It was written that you would have duck, spuds and a bottle of wine. (*She goes.*)

JACQUES: Sir. You were going to say a word on the subject of this poet.

MASTER: (*Still under the spell of the* INNKEEPER) Poet?

JACQUES: The young poet who went to find our master.

MASTER: Oh yes. One day, a young poet came to our master's place – the master who invented us. They often used to come and annoy him. Young poets are always legion. They multiply at a rate of about four hundred thousand a year. In

France alone. And it's even worse in less cultured countries.

JACQUES: What can be done about it? Drown them?

MASTER: That was the practice in the past. In Sparta, in the good old days. There poets were hurled into the sea from the top of a cliff as soon as possible after birth. In our enlightened century, however, anyone at all can live to the end of their natural span.

INNKEEPER: (*Bringing a bottle of wine and filling glasses*) Like it?

MASTER: (*Having tasted the wine*) Excellent. Leave the bottle. (INNKEEPER *goes.*) Now, one day, a young poet showed up at our master's and pulled some paper out of his pocket. 'Surprise, surprise,' said our master, 'poems!' 'Yes, Master, poems, my own, original poems,' said the poet. 'I want you to tell me the truth, nothing but the truth.' – 'And you aren't afraid of the truth?' said our master. 'No,' replied the young poet in a trembling voice. And our master said to him, 'Dear young friend, not only have you proved to me that your poems are not worth their own weight in shit, you have shown beyond question that you will never write better ones.' 'That's annoying,' says the young poet, 'it means I shall have to write bad poems all my life.' And our master replied, 'A warning, young poet. Neither the gods, nor men, nor the signposts in the street, have ever forgiven mediocrity in a poet!' 'I know,' says the poet, 'but there's nothing I can do about it. It's an impulse.'

JACQUES: A what?

MASTER: An impulse. 'I have this terrific impulse that drives me to write bad poems.' 'Again, I warn you!' cried our master; and the young poet replied, 'I know, Master, that you are the great Diderot, and that I am a bad poet, but we bad poets, there are more of us than you, we're always going to be in the majority. All of humanity is made up of nothing but bad poets. And the public, in its mind, its taste and its feelings, is just a huge gathering of bad poets. How would a bad poet give offence to other bad poets? The bad poets who constitute the human race adore bad poetry. It's

precisely because I write such bad poems that one day I'll
be established as a great poet.'

JACQUES: That's what that bad young man said to our master?

MASTER: Word for word.

JACQUES: What he said is not without a certain truth.

MASTER: Absolutely not. And it has led me to formulate a
blasphemous thought.

JACQUES: I know the one you mean.

MASTER: You know the one I mean?

JACQUES: I know it.

MASTER: Say it then.

JACQUES: No, no, you thought of it first.

MASTER: You had it at the same time, don't lie.

JACQUES: I had it after you.

MASTER: All right, fine, what is the thought? Come on! Out
with it!

JACQUES: The thought has come to you that maybe our master
was perhaps himself a bad poet.

MASTER: And who can prove that he wasn't?

JACQUES: Do you think we'd be better if someone else had
invented us?

MASTER: (*Dreamily*) It depends. If we'd come from the pen of a
really great writer, a genius . . . yes. Definitely.

JACQUES: (*Sadly, after a pause*) You know what's sad?

MASTER: No, I don't know what's sad. What is sad?

JACQUES: What's sad is that you should have such a poor
opinion of your creator.

MASTER: (*Looking at* JACQUES) I judge the creator by his work.

JACQUES: We should love our master who made us what we are.
We would be happier if we loved him. We would be calmer
and more sure of ourselves. Not you. You want a better
creator. Frankly, Master, that's blasphemy.

INNKEEPER: (*Bringing the food on a dish*) The duck, gentlemen
. . . when you've finished, I'll tell you the tale of Mme de
La Pommeraye.

JACQUES: (*Displeased*) As it happens, when we've finished *I* will
be telling the story of how I fell in love.

INNKEEPER: It's up to your master to say who tells what.
MASTER: Oh no! Not me! It depends on what's been written up there.
INNKEEPER: It's written up there that it's my turn.

SCENE ONE

Same setting: the stage is totally empty except for a table downstage at which JACQUES *and his* MASTER *are seated, finishing their supper.*

JACQUES: It all started with my losing my cherry. I got pissed, my dad hit me round the head, a regiment was passing by . . .

INNKEEPER: (*Coming in*) Good, was it?

MASTER: Delicious!

JACQUES: Excellent!

INNKEEPER: 'Nother bottle?

MASTER: Why not?

INNKEEPER: (*To the wings*) Another bottle! (*To* JACQUES *and his* MASTER) I promised the gentlemen to tell them the tale of Mme de La Pommeraye after dinner . . .

JACQUES: God in heaven! Lady! I'm in the middle of telling how I fell in love!

INNKEEPER: Men fall in love very easily, and just as easily drop you. Everyone knows that. I am now going to tell you a story that will teach you that the buggers get punished in the end.

JACQUES: You're all mouth, aren't you, mine hostess? You've got eighteen thousand tons of words down that throat of yours, and you lie in waiting for some poor bloody ear that you can empty 'em all into.

INNKEEPER: That's what I call a badly brought up servant, sir. He thinks it's funny to keep interrupting a lady.

MASTER: (*Reprovingly*) Jacques, you're getting above yourself . . .

INNKEEPER: So, there was this Marquis, name of Des Arcis. A real laugh, always after the girls. A really nice guy. No respect for women, though.

JACQUES: Quite right.

INNKEEPER: Monsewer Jacques. Interrupting.

JACQUES: Mine Hostess of the Stag, I was not talking to you.

INNKEEPER: So this Marquis had ferreted out a certain
    Marquise de La Pommeraye. A widow who from childhood
    carried herself off as befits a woman of wealth and rank. It
    took time and effort on the part of the Marquis to get her to
    give in and make him happy. After a few years, however,
    the Marquis started getting bored. You see what I'm
    saying, gentlemen. First of all, he suggested that he should
    get out a bit more often. Then that she should entertain
    more. Next he stopped going to her place even when she
    had visitors. He always had something pressing to do.
    When he did go, he hardly said a word, sprawled in an
    armchair, picked up a book, chucked it down, played with
    the dog and fell asleep in front of her. But Mme the
    Marquise still loved him and suffered dreadfully. And
    being proud, she got pissed off, and decided to put an end
    to it.

SCENE TWO

During the INNKEEPER's *last speech, the* MARQUIS *comes on,
carrying a chair which he puts down and lolls lazily on, with a
saintly expression on his face.*

INNKEEPER: (*turning to the* MARQUIS) My friend . . .

A VOICE: (*Offstage*) Service!

INNKEEPER: (*Into the wings*) What?

VOICE: The pantry key!

INNKEEPER: It's on the nail . . . (*To the* MARQUIS) You're
    dreaming, my friend . . .
    (*She climbs on to the rostrum and approaches the* MARQUIS.)

MARQUIS: You too, Marquise, are dreaming.

INNKEEPER: I am; rather sadly, too.

MARQUIS: What's troubling you?

INNKEEPER: Nothing.

MARQUIS: (*Yawning*) That's not true! Come on, tell me about it; at least it'll dispel our boredom.

INNKEEPER: You're bored, are you?

MARQUIS: No, no! . . . But there are days when . . .

INNKEEPER: When we bore each other?

MARQUIS: No! You misunderstand, dearest . . . But some days . . . God alone knows why . . .

INNKEEPER: Dear friend, for some time I've wanted to tell you a secret. But I fear distressing you.

MARQUIS: Could you ever distress me? You?

INNKEEPER: God knows I'd rather do anything but that.

VOICE: (*From the wings*) Service!

INNKEEPER: (*To the wings*) I've already told you to stop pestering me. Ask the boss!

VOICE: He's not there!

INNKEEPER: What the fuck's it got to do with me?

VOICE: It's the straw salesman.

INNKEEPER: Pay him and tell him to piss off . . . (*To the* MARQUIS) Yes, Marquis, it came about without my knowledge and it has devastated me. Last night, I questioned myself and said: is the Marquis less worthy of love than before? Do I have anything to reproach him with? Would he be unfaithful? No! So why has my heart changed, while his has remained constant? I no longer experience the same anxiety when he arrives late, nor do I feel so sweetly happy when he appears.

MARQUIS: (*Joyfully*) Really?

INNKEEPER: Marquis, spare me your reproaches . . . or rather, don't spare me. I deserve them . . . should I have concealed all this? I'm the one who's changed, not you . . . which is why I respect you more than ever. I refuse to lie to myself. Love has left my heart. It's a terrible thing to find out, but it is none the less true.

MARQUIS: (*Happily flinging himself to the ground*) You are utterly charming, the most charming creature in the world.

The happiness you've given me! Your frankness shames me. You're so much better than me! I'm so small next to you. You see, your heart's history is word for word my heart's history – except that I never had the courage to say it.

INNKEEPER: Truly?

MARQUIS: As true as true can be. We should just rejoice at having ceased feeling the same fragile, deceptive emotion which was binding us together at exactly the same time.

INNKEEPER: Yes: it's terribly sad when one person loves while the other feels love no more.

MARQUIS: Never have you looked lovelier to me than you do now. Had experience not taught me caution, I should say that I love you now more than ever.

INNKEEPER: Marquis: what shall we do?

MARQUIS: We have neither lied nor deceived each other. You are entitled to all my respect, and I don't think I've entirely forfeited yours. We can be the best of friends. We'll support each other during our intrigues. Who knows what might not happen . . .

JACQUES: My God, who knows . . .

VOICE: (*Backstage*) Where's my old woman?

INNKEEPER: (*Vexed, into the wings*) What you want?

VOICE: (*Backstage*) Nuffink!

INNKEEPER: (*To* JACQUES *and his* MASTER) Drive you potty, it would. Just when you think it's quiet in this hole, everyone asleep, he has to shout out. The old pig's made me lose my thread . . .
(*She comes down.*)
Gents, you should really pity me.

SCENE THREE

MASTER: Oh I pity you, Madame. (*Pats her on the bum*) At the same time, I congratulate you: you know how to tell a tale

49

all right. I've just had an extraordinary idea. What would happen if you were married, not to your husband, whom you just described as an old pig, but to Monsieur Jacques here? To put it another way, what would a husband incapable of shutting up do with a wife who couldn't stop chattering?

JACQUES: I'll tell you: he would do exactly what they did to me all the years I lived with my grandpa and grandma. They were very serious people. They got up, dressed, went to work. They had lunch, and then they went back to work. At night grandma used to sew and grandpa read the Bible, and no one opened their mouth all day long.

MASTER: What did you do?

JACQUES: I sat in the room with a gag on my mouth.

INNKEEPER: A gag?

JACQUES: Grandpa was fond of silence. Which meant that I spent my first twelve years gagged.

INNKEEPER: (*To the wings*) Jean?

VOICE: (*In the wings*) What?

INNKEEPER: Two bottles! Not the stuff we give customers. The good stuff, right at the bottom, behind the wood.

VOICE: Got you.

INNKEEPER: Monsieur Jacques, I've changed my mind about you. You're a very touching person. I can just see you with a gag round your mouth, and you've got this terrible desire to talk, and – suddenly I feel great love for you. Let's make it up. (*They kiss.*)
(WAITER *comes on and puts two bottles on the table, opens them and fills three glasses.*)

INNKEEPER: Gentlemen, you will never taste better wine all your life!

JACQUES: Innkeeper, you must have been one hell of a tasty woman!

MASTER: She *is* one hell of a tasty woman, you cad.

INNKEEPER: Not what I was, of course. Should've seen me before! But we're drifting ... back to Mme de La Pommeraye ...

JACQUES: First, let's drink to all the heads you've turned!

INNKEEPER: Why not? (*They clink glasses and drink.*) Back to Mme de La Pommeraye.

JACQUES: Not before having drunk the Marquis's health: I'm worried about him.

INNKEEPER: So you should be.

(*More clinking and drinking.*)

SCENE FOUR

During the last speeches of the previous scene, the MOTHER *and the* DAUGHTER *come on to the rostrum from the back of the stage.*

INNKEEPER: Can't you imagine her fury? She tells the Marquis that she doesn't love him, and he frolics for joy! This is a proud lady, gents. (*Turns towards the* MOTHER *and the* DAUGHTER.) She ran into these two creatures again. She'd known them before. The Mother and the Daughter. A court case had brought them to Paris: they lost it and were ruined. The mother was reduced to running a gambling-den.

MOTHER: (*From the top of the rostrum*) Needs must. I tried to get my girl into the Opera. Is it my fault that the silly goose's got a voice like a rusty hinge?

INNKEEPER: The gambling-den was frequented by men who would gamble, have some supper, and then one or two of them would generally stay on and sleep with either the mother or the daughter. They were really just ...

JACQUES: Yes, they were just ... but let's drink to them all the same.

(JACQUES *raises his glass; they clink and drink.*)

MOTHER: (*Addressing the* INNKEEPER) To be candid, Mme la Marquise, we pursue a delicate and risky profession.

INNKEEPER: (*Going towards them on the rostrum*) I hope you are not too well known in this profession?

MOTHER: Happily, I think not. Our ... business ... is in the rue Hambourg ... far enough outside of ...

INNKEEPER: I imagine you're not especially attached to this profession? Should I suggest a somewhat brighter lot in life for you, might you go along with it?

MOTHER: (*Gratefully*) Oh, Mme la Marquise!

INNKEEPER: But you must do as I say to the last particular.

MOTHER: Count on us.

INNKEEPER: Good. Go home. Sell your furniture. And get rid of those clothes which are a touch on the loud side.

JACQUES: (*Raising his glass*) To the young lady's health. She has a melancholy look about her, no doubt from changing men every night.

INNKEEPER: (*To* JACQUES, *from the top of the rostrum*) It's not a laughing matter. If only you knew just how revolting it can be, sometimes. (*To the two ladies*) I'm going to take a small flat for you. I shall furnish it as soberly as possible. You will only leave it in order to go to church and back. In the street your eyes will always be lowered, and you will never go out without each other. You will speak only of God. I, needless to say, will never visit you. I am unworthy ... of the company of such saintly women ... now, run along, do exactly as I've said!

(*The two women leave.*)

MASTER: This woman frightens me.

INNKEEPER: (*To the* MASTER, *from the back of the stage*) And you hardly know her yet.

SCENE FIVE

The MARQUIS *comes on from the side of the stage. He lightly touches the* INNKEEPER's *arm. She turns to him with a surprised expression.*

INNKEEPER: Marquis! I'm delighted to see you! How are your adventures going? Those budding young maidens of yours? (*The* MARQUIS *takes her by the arm; together they walk up*

and down, while he leans towards her, from time to time
whispering into her ear.)
MASTER: He's telling her everything! Blind pig!
INNKEEPER: I do admire you. (*The* MARQUIS *murmurs into her*
ear again.) Always so successful with women!
MARQUIS: What about you? Have you nothing to tell me? (*The*
INNKEEPER *shakes her head.*) What about that little count,
the dwarf, the midget, who's so keen to . . .
INNKEEPER: I no longer see him.
MARQUIS: Oh come on! You've rejected the dwarf?
INNKEEPER: He displeases me.
MARQUIS: How can he not please you? He's the most adorable
dwarf in the world! . . . You're not . . . still in love with *me?*
INNKEEPER: It could be.
MARQUIS: You're expecting me to come back to you and are
storing up for yourself all the advantages of spotless
conduct.
INNKEEPER: Does that worry you?
MARQUIS: What a dangerous woman you are!
(*The* MARQUIS *and the* INNKEEPER *promenade up and down*
the rostrum; another couple come up to them: the MOTHER *and*
the DAUGHTER.)
INNKEEPER: (*Feigning surprise*) My God, can it be possible?
(*Lets go of the* MARQUIS's *arm and goes towards the two*
women) Is it you, Madame?
MOTHER: Yes, it's me . . .
INNKEEPER: How are you? What's happened to you all this
time?
MOTHER: You know our misfortunes. We live modestly and in
seclusion.
INNKEEPER: I approve of your secluded lives, but why did you
cut yourself off from me – I who –
DAUGHTER: Madame, I mentioned you to mother a dozen
times, but she always said 'Mme de La Pommeraye? She
will certainly have forgotten us.'
INNKEEPER: How unfair! I'm delighted to see you. This is the
Marquis des Arcis. His presence will not embarrass you.

How tall you've grown, young lady!
(*All four start walking again.*)

MASTER: You know, Jacques, I like this innkeeper. I'll wager she wasn't born in this inn. She's out of its class. I have insight into these things.

INNKEEPER: No, really! How beautiful you've become, young lady!

MASTER: Say what you like, this is a noble woman.

MARQUIS: (*To the two women*) Stay a little! Don't go!

MOTHER: (*Timidly*) No, no . . . we have to go to vespers . . . come on, miss!
(*They bow and rush off.*)

MARQUIS: God, Marquise, who are those women?

INNKEEPER: The happiest creatures I know. You observed their calmness? Their serenity? It seems that there's great wisdom in a secluded life.

MARQUIS: Marquise, I should be filled with remorse if I thought our separation would lead you to such sad extremes.

INNKEEPER: Would you prefer me to entertain the little count again?

MARQUIS: The midget? Certainly.

INNKEEPER: That's your advice?

MARQUIS: Unhesitating.
(INNKEEPER *comes off the rostrum.*)

INNKEEPER: (*To* JACQUES *and his* MASTER, *indignantly*) You hear?
(*She takes a glass from the table and drinks. Then she sits on the edge of the rostrum. The* MARQUIS *sits next to her. She carries on:*)
This ages me! When I first saw her, she was no more than three apples high.

MARQUIS: You mean the lady's daughter?

INNKEEPER: Yes. When I saw her I felt like a blown rose next to one in bud. You noticed her?

MARQUIS: Of course.

INNKEEPER: What did you think?

MARQUIS: I'd say she was like a Raphael Virgin.

INNKEEPER: That expression!

MARQUIS: The voice!

INNKEEPER: The skin!

MARQUIS: The smile!

JACQUES: For God's sake, Marquis, if you go on like that, you'll never get out of it!

INNKEEPER: (*To* JACQUES) I believe you: he'll never get out of it!
(*She gets up, takes her glass and drinks.*)

MARQUIS: The body!
(*With these words, he gets up and leaves, walking in an arc across the rostrum.*)

INNKEEPER: (*To* JACQUES *and his* MASTER) He's risen to the bait.

JACQUES: Mine hostess, this Marquise is a monster.

INNKEEPER: And the Marquis? He only had to stop not loving her!

JACQUES: Mine hostess, no doubt you are unfamiliar with the charming fable of the Sheath and the Cutlass.

MASTER: You've never told me that one . . .

SCENE SIX

The MARQUIS *walks in an arc towards the* INNKEEPER *and speaks to her in a begging voice.*

MARQUIS: Well, Marquise, have you seen your lady friends?

INNKEEPER: (*To* JACQUES *and his* MASTER) You see how caught he is?

MARQUIS: That's not very kind of you! They're so poor, and you never even invite them to have a meal with you.

INNKEEPER: I invite them, but in vain. It's not surprising: if they were seen to be visiting me, everyone would say they were under the protection of the Marquise de La

Pommeraye, and all the charity they receive would come to an end.

MARQUIS: What! They live on charity!

INNKEEPER: Yes, on the charity of their parish.

MARQUIS: They're your friends, and they have to live on charity!

INNKEEPER: Ah, Marquis, we are far, we men and women of the world, from understanding the delicate sensibilities of pious people. They don't accept help from just anyone. Only from hands which are pure and without blemish.

MARQUIS: Do you know, I'm tempted to call on them.

INNKEEPER: You would risk them losing everything. With that young lady's charms it would need no more than a visit to set tongues wagging.

MARQUIS: (*With a sigh*) It's cruel.

INNKEEPER: (*With double meaning*) Yes, cruel. That's the word.

MARQUIS: Marquise, you're mocking me.

INNKEEPER: I'm trying rather to protect you from great unhappiness. Because, Marquis, you are preparing great torments for yourself. You're going to confuse this young girl with all the other women you've known. This young girl is not going to let herself be tempted like all the others. You are not going to get what you want.
(*The* MARQUIS *heads for the back of the stage with a weary air.*)

JACQUES: This Marquise is really naughty.

INNKEEPER: (*To* JACQUES) Don't defend men, Monsieur Jacques. Have you forgotten quite how much Mme de La Pommeraye loved the Marquis? She's still madly in love with him. Each of his words is a dagger thrust into her heart. Can't you see that what she's doing is setting up a hell for both of them?
(MARQUIS *semi-circles back to the* INNKEEPER. *She looks at him.*)
My God, you look dreadful!

MARQUIS: (*Pacing up and down the stage*) I'm haunted. I can't stand it any more. I can't sleep. I can't eat. For a fortnight I've drunk like a fish then I've prayed like a monk, in the

hope of catching a glimpse of her in church . . . Marquise,
you must make it possible for me to see her!
(MARQUISE *sighs*.)
You are my one friend!

INNKEEPER: I would gladly help you, Marquis, but it's
difficult. She mustn't think that I'm in cahoots with
you . . .

MARQUIS: I beg you!

INNKEEPER: (*Imitating him*) I beg you! . . . what does it matter
to me whether you're in love or not? Why should I
complicate my life? It's your problem.

MARQUIS: I implore you! If you desert me, I'm lost. If you
can't do it for my sake, do it for theirs! I can't answer for
myself any longer. I'll smash their door down and you
don't know what I'm capable of!

INNKEEPER: As you wish. But at the very least, give me time to
prepare . . .
(*At the back of the stage, the servants have put chairs and a
table in place. The* MARQUIS *goes out*.)

SCENE SEVEN

INNKEEPER: (*Upstage, where the* MOTHER *and* DAUGHTER *are
entering*) Good, come on, come on. Stand with me and we'll
start. (*They sit at the table, upstage. There are now two tables
on stage: the lower one, where* JACQUES *and his* MASTER *are
sitting, the higher one on the rostrum*.)

JACQUES: (*Calling out to the* INNKEEPER) Mine hostess! This
woman is a bitch!

INNKEEPER: And the Marquis, Monsieur Jacques? Angel, is
he?

JACQUES: Why should he be an angel? Has man no choice but
to be angel or animal? You would no doubt be wiser if
you were acquainted with the fable of the Sheath and the
Cutlass.

MARQUIS: (*Approaching the women, feigns surprise*) Oh! . . . I'm
    afraid I'm disturbing you.
INNKEEPER: (*Equally surprised*) Indeed . . . we were not
    expecting you, Marquis.
MASTER: Such actors!
INNKEEPER: But since you're here, please dine with us.
    (MARQUIS *kisses the ladies' hands and sits down.*)
JACQUES: I'm sure this isn't going to interest you much. I'll tell
    you the fable of the Sheath and the Cutlass.
MARQUIS: (*Joining in the ladies' conversation*) I couldn't agree
    with you more. What are life's pleasures? Dust and smoke.
    Do you know the man I admire above all others?
JACQUES: Don't listen, sir!
MARQUIS: You don't know? I'll tell you: St Simon Stylites. My
    patron saint.
JACQUES: The fable of the Sheath and the Cutlass is the moral
    of morals, and the foundation of all knowledge.
MARQUIS: Imagine, ladies! Simon spent forty years of his life
    on a forty-foot column praying to God!
JACQUES: Listen. The Sheath and the Cutlass were fighting like
    rag-and-bone men. Cutlass said to Sheath: Sheath, my love,
    you're a real whore, every day you get entered by another
    cutlass. And Sheath replied to Cutlass: Cutlass, my love,
    you're a right bastard, because you change sheaths every
    day.
MARQUIS: Imagine, ladies, forty years of his life on a forty-foot
    column!
JACQUES: This row took place at table. And the person who was
    sitting between Sheath and Cutlass, said the following: My
    dear Sheath, and you, my dear Cutlass, you can easily
    change sheaths and cutlasses, but you will have made a
    grave mistake the day that you promise not to change any
    more. Do you not know, Cutlass, that God made you to
    penetrate many sheaths?
DAUGHTER: This column was really forty foot high?
JACQUES: And you, Sheath, have you not learned that God
    made you for many cutlasses?

(MASTER *has listened to* JACQUES *without looking at the rostrum. After these last words, he laughs.*)

MARQUIS: (*With amorous tenderness*) Yes, child. Forty foot high.

DAUGHTER: And Simon didn't get giddy?

MARQUIS: No. He was not giddy. And do you know why, child?

DAUGHTER: No.

MARQUIS: Because from the heights of his column, he never looked down. His eyes were perpetually trained on God, towards the heights. And whoever looks up to the heights, can never get giddy.

LADIES: How true!

MASTER: Jacques!

JACQUES: Yes.

MARQUIS: (*Taking leave of the ladies*) This has been a great honour for me.

MASTER: (*Amused*) Your fable is immoral. I reject it, I deny it, and I declare it null and void.

JACQUES: But you liked it!

MASTER: That's not the point! Who wouldn't like it? Of course it pleased me!
(*Upstage, the servants have taken the table and chairs away.* JACQUES *and his* MASTER *look at the rostrum again. The* MARQUIS *approaches the* INNKEEPER.)

SCENE EIGHT

INNKEEPER: Well, Marquis, could you find a woman in the whole of France who would do for you what I have done?

MARQUIS: (*Kneeling at her feet*) You are my only friend . . .

INNKEEPER: Let's change the subject. What does your heart say?

MARQUIS: I must have that girl or I'll burst.

INNKEEPER: I would be very happy to save your life.

MARQUIS: I know this is going to annoy you, but I have to tell you: I have sent them a letter, and a box of jewels. But they sent them back – both of them.

INNKEEPER: (*Severely*) Love is corrupting you, Marquis. What have these poor women done to you to deserve being dirtied? You think virtue can be bought for a few stones?

MARQUIS: (*Still on his knees*) Forgive me.

INNKEEPER: I anticipated you. You are incorrigible.

MARQUIS: Dear friend. I want to make one last attempt. I'm going to make over to them one of my houses in town and another in the country. I'm going to give them half of all I own.

INNKEEPER: As you please . . . But honour has no price. I know these women.
(*She goes towards the* MARQUIS. *He remains on his knees on the stage. Having come from the other side of the stage, the* MOTHER *goes towards the* INNKEEPER *and kneels in front of her.*)

MOTHER: Mme la Marquise! Allow us not to refuse this offer! Such a great fortune! Such great wealth! Such a great honour!

INNKEEPER: (*To the* MOTHER, *still on her knees*) You imagine that what I did was done to make you happy? You will now go immediately and refuse the Marquis's offer.

JACQUES: What more does she want, this woman?

INNKEEPER: (*To* JACQUES) What does she want? Certainly not the good of these women. They mean nothing to her, Monsieur Jacques! (*To the* MOTHER) Either do as I tell you, or I shall send you straight back to your brothel!
(*She turns her back on them and finds herself face to face with the* MARQUIS, *who is still on his knees.*)

MARQUIS: You are right, dear friend. They refused. I am in despair. What should I do? You know what I've determined on, Marquise? I shall marry her.

INNKEEPER: (*Feigning surprise*) Marquis, this is a serious matter which requires mature reflection.

MARQUIS: What's the use of reflection! I can hardly be
    unhappier than I am!
INNKEEPER: Gently, now, Marquis. We're talking about your
    whole life. You shouldn't be hasty. (*Pretending to think
    about it*) These women are virtuous, that's certain. Their
    heart is pure as snow . . . perhaps you're right. Poverty is
    not a vice.
MARQUIS: Go and see them, I beg you. And inform them of my
    intentions.
    (INNKEEPER *turns toward the* MARQUIS *and extends her
    hand to him; she makes him stand up, and they are now facing
    each other; she smiles.*)
INNKEEPER: Very well, I promise.
MARQUIS: Thank you.
INNKEEPER: What would I not do for you.
MARQUIS: (*Suddenly euphoric*) But tell me, you who are my one
    real friend, why don't you get married too?
INNKEEPER: To whom, Marquis?
MARQUIS: To the little count.
INNKEEPER: That dwarf?
MARQUIS: He's rich, witty . . .
INNKEEPER: And who will guarantee his faithfulness to me?
    You, perhaps?
MARQUIS: Faithfulness in a husband is easily dispensed with.
INNKEEPER: Not to me. It would offend me. Besides, I am of a
    vengeful nature.
MARQUIS: If you're of a vengeful nature, we'll revenge you.
    That wouldn't be too bad. I tell you what: we'll rent a
    palace for the four of us and be happier than a club with
    four leaves.
INNKEEPER: That wouldn't be bad, no.
MARQUIS: If your dwarf annoys you, we'll put him in a vase on
    your bedside table.
INNKEEPER: Your proposal is very attractive, but I shall not
    marry. The only man I could ever marry . . .
MARQUIS: Is me?
INNKEEPER: I can now admit it without fear.

MARQUIS: Why didn't you tell me earlier?

INNKEEPER: From what I can see, I've done the right thing. Who you have chosen will suit you better than me.

(*The* DAUGHTER *advances from the back of the stage in her white bridal gown. The* MARQUIS *goes to meet her as if in a trance.*)

MARQUIS: Marquise, I will be beholden to you for the rest of my days . . .

(*He goes slowly to meet the* DAUGHTER. *They kiss and will remain in each other's arms for a long time.*)

SCENE NINE

The INNKEEPER, *while the* MARQUIS *and the* DAUGHTER *prolong their embrace, slowly walks backwards, never taking her eyes off them, till she reaches the back of the rostrum. Then she says to the* MARQUIS:

INNKEEPER: Marquis!

(*The* MARQUIS *hardly hears her words, entwined as he still is with the* DAUGHTER.)

INNKEEPER: Marquis! (*The* MARQUIS *slightly moves his head in her direction.*) Was your wedding night to your satisfaction?

JACQUES: Jesus! What!

INNKEEPER: I'm happy to hear it. Now: listen to me. You had an honest woman that you didn't know how to keep. That woman was me. (JACQUES *starts laughing.*) I've taken my revenge on you by making you marry someone worthy of you. Go to the rue Hambourg and you'll discover how this woman used to earn her living! Your wife and your mother-in-law!

(*The* INNKEEPER *roars with satanic laughter. The* DAUGHTER *throws herself at the* MARQUIS's *feet.*)

MARQUIS: Wretch, wretch . . .

DAUGHTER: (*At his feet*) Marquis, trample on me, wipe me
    cut . . .
MARQUIS: Get away from me, wretch . . .
DAUGHTER: Do with me what you will . . .
INNKEEPER: Run, Marquis! Run to the rue Hambourg! And
    when you get there put up a commemorative plaque: Here
    Whored the Marquis des Arcis.
    (*More satanic laughter from the* INNKEEPER)
DAUGHTER: (*On the ground, at the* MARQUIS's *feet*) Monsieur,
    have pity on me . . .
    (*The* MARQUIS *pushes her away with his foot, the* DAUGHTER
    tries to hold on to his leg, but he pulls himself away. The
    DAUGHTER *stays on the ground.*)
JACQUES: Hostess! That can't be the end of the story!
INNKEEPER: Sure it is. I wouldn't risk adding what might be to
    it, if I were you.
    (JACQUES *leaps on to the rostrum and stands exactly where a
    moment ago the* MARQUIS *was: the* DAUGHTER *wraps herself
    around his legs.*)
DAUGHTER: Monsieur le Marquis, let me at least hope for your
    pardon!
JACQUES: Get up!
DAUGHTER: (*On the ground, grabs him by the legs*) Do with me
    what you will, I'll submit to anything at all.
JACQUES: (*His voice sincere and emotional*) Get up, I tell you . . .
    (*The* DAUGHTER *doesn't dare to do so.*) Many honest girls
    become dishonest women. Why shouldn't the opposite
    happen for once? (*Tenderly*) I am moreover convinced that
    your debauchery has merely enhanced your loveliness. It
    never so much as reached it. Get up. You hear me? I have
    forgiven you. At the worst, most shameful moment, I never
    ceased to think of you as my wife. Be honest, be faithful, be
    happy, and make me all of those things. I ask no more of
    you. Get up, wife. Madame la Marquise, get up! Get up,
    Mme des Arcis.
    (*The* DAUGHTER *gets up, hugs* JACQUES *and kisses him with
    abandon.*)

INNKEEPER: (*Shouting from the other side of the stage*) She's a *whore*, Marquis!

JACQUES: I should watch your mouth, Mme de La Pommeraye! (*To the* DAUGHTER) I have forgiven you, and it is very important to me that you understand that I have no regrets. This woman (*Indicates the* INNKEEPER) instead of revenging herself on me, has performed me a great service. Are you not younger than she, more beautiful, and a hundred times more devout? We shall now leave together for the country where we shall live for many happy years. (*He crosses the rostrum with her, then turns to the* INNKEEPER, *dropping the role of the* MARQUIS.) And I may tell you, mine hostess, that they were very happy. Because nothing is certain in this world, and things change meaning as the wind blows. And the wind never stops blowing, and you never even know it. And the wind blows and happiness turns to unhappiness and vengeance to reward, and a loose girl becomes a wife faithful beyond compare . . .

SCENE TEN

During JACQUES's *last few speeches, the* INNKEEPER *comes down from the rostrum and sits at the table where* JACQUES *and his* MASTER *sit; the* MASTER *grabs her by the waist and drinks with her.*

MASTER: Jacques, I don't like the way you ended that story! That girl didn't deserve to become a Marquise! She reminds me terribly of Agathe. Scheming bitches, both of them.

JACQUES: You're wrong, Master.

MASTER: What! Me, wrong?

JACQUES: You're very gravely wrong.

MASTER: Someone called Jacques is going to give *me*, his master, lessons? Going to *explain* to *me* whether I'm right or wrong?
(JACQUES *releases the* DAUGHTER, *who withdraws during the remaining dialogue and leaps off the rostrum in one.*)
JACQUES: I am not someone-called-Jacques. I would like to remind you that you called me your friend, as a matter of fact.
MASTER: (*Touching up the* INNKEEPER) Should I wish to call you my friend, you will be my friend. And should I wish to call you someone-called-Jacques, you will be someone-called-Jacques. Because, up there, you know, up there! as your old captain would say, up there it is written that I am your master. And I order you to withdraw the ending of that story which displeases me, as indeed it displeases Madame the Marquise de La Pommeraye, whom I revere (*Kisses the* INNKEEPER) because she is a noble lady who has a magnificent arse . . .
JACQUES: You really think, Master, that Jacques can withdraw the story that he's told?
MASTER: If his master wishes it, Jacques will withdraw his story!
JACQUES: I'd like to see that, really, I would. Sir.
MASTER: (*Still fondling the* INNKEEPER) If Jacques continues to be obstinate, his master will have to send him to the stable, to sleep with the goats!
JACQUES: I won't go!
MASTER: (*Kissing the* INNKEEPER) You'll go.
JACQUES: I won't go.
MASTER: (*Shouting*) You will go!
INNKEEPER: Sir, could you possibly do something for the lady you've just kissed?
MASTER: For that lady, anything.
INNKEEPER: Stop quarrelling with your servant. I do see that he's particularly insolent, but I think you need a servant exactly like him. It is written up there that you can't get by without each other.

MASTER: (*To* JACQUES) You hear that, valet? Mme de La
      Pommeraye has just said that I shall never be able to get rid
      of you.
JACQUES: You are going to be able to get rid of me, Master,
      because I'm going to sleep in the stable with the goats.
MASTER: (*Rising*) You won't go!
JACQUES: I will go. (*Leaves slowly*)
MASTER: You will not go!
JACQUES: I'll go.
MASTER: Jacques! (JACQUES *goes slowly, more and more slowly.*)
      Little Jacques! (JACQUES *keeps going . . .*) My dear little
      Jacques . . . (*the* MASTER *runs after him, grabs him by the
      arm.*) Come on now, you heard. What would I do without
      you?
JACQUES: All right. But to avoid rows in future, we should
      come to an agreement on certain basic principles once and
      for all.
MASTER: I'm in favour of that.
JACQUES: Let's lay them down. Since it is written up there that
      I'm indispensable to you, I will take advantage of that fact
      on every possible occasion.
MASTER: That's not written up there!
JACQUES: All of that was stipulated the moment our Master
      invented us. He decided that you would have appearances
      and I would have substance. That you would give the
      orders, but I would choose which ones to obey. That you
      would have the power but I would have the influence.
MASTER: If that's the way things are, we'll swap. I'll take your
      place.
JACQUES: You wouldn't gain anything from it. You would lose
      the appearance but have no substance. You would lose
      power without gaining influence. Stay as you are, Master.
      If you're a good master, an obedient master, you'll find
      things won't get any worse.
MASTER: Amen. The sky's black and it is written up there that
      we have drunk a great deal and that we are going to go to
      bed.

ACT THREE

SCENE ONE

The stage is totally empty. The MASTER *and* JACQUES *are on the apron.*

MASTER: But tell me where our horses are.

JACQUES: Leave off the stupid questions, if you please, sir.

MASTER: I mean, it's rubbish! As if a Frenchman could cross France on foot! Do you know this person who's been allowed to rewrite our story?

JACQUES: A halfwit, sir. But now that it's been rewritten, it can't be changed again.

MASTER: Death to people who rewrite what's already been written! I'd like to see them skewered and barbecued. They should have their balls and their ears cut off. My feet hurt.

JACQUES: Sir, people who rewrite are never barbecued, and everyone believes them.

MASTER: You think they'll believe the person who's rewritten our story? They won't look up the text to find out who we really are?

JACQUES: Sir, ours isn't the first story to be rewritten. Every single thing that's ever happened down here has already been rewritten hundreds of times, and no one would ever dream of checking what really happened. The history of mankind has been rewritten so often that people don't know who they are any more.

MASTER: You frighten me. So these people (*Indicates the audience*) are going to believe that we didn't even have horses, and that we had to go through our story like barefoot tramps?

JACQUES: (*Indicates the audience*) Them? You can make *them* believe anything.

MASTER: You seem grumpy today. We should've stayed at the Stag.

JACQUES: I wouldn't have said no.

MASTER: Nevertheless . . . that woman wasn't born in an inn. I told you so.

JACQUES: Where, then?

MASTER: I don't know. But that diction! That charm . . .

JACQUES: It seems to me, Master, that you're falling in love.

MASTER: (*Shrugging*) If it was written up there . . . (*After a pause*) which reminds me: you never finished telling me how you fell in love.

JACQUES: There was no need to give Mme de La Pommeraye's story precedence yesterday.

MASTER: Yesterday, I gave precedence to a great lady. You'll never understand gallantry, will you? Today, as we're alone, I give you precedence.

JACQUES: Thank you. Very much. Now, listen. When I lost my cherry, I got pissed. When I got pissed, my old dad bashed me round the head. When my old dad bashed me round the head, I signed up . . .

MASTER: You're repeating yourself, Jacques.

JACQUES: Me? Repeating myself? Really sir, there is nothing more shameful than to repeat oneself. That's something you shouldn't say, you know. Right. That's it. I'm not opening my mouth till the end of the show . . .

MASTER: Jacques, I beg you.

JACQUES: Oh you're begging me, are you? Begging me, now?

MASTER: Yes.

JACQUES: Right. Now, where was I?

MASTER: Your old dad bashed you over the head. You signed on, and eventually you found yourself in front of a shack where they looked after you and where there was this very pretty woman with a large bottom . . . (*Interrupting himself*) Jacques . . . now Jacques, frankly, now, I mean *really* frankly . . . this woman – did she really have a big bottom, or are you just saying it to make me happy . . ?

JACQUES: Why are you asking these useless questions, sir?

MASTER: (*With melancholy*) She didn't, did she? Have a big arse?

JACQUES: (*Sweetly*) Don't ask, sir. You know I hate lying to
you.
MASTER: (*Still melancholy*) See – you've misled me, Jacques.
JACQUES: Don't be cross with me.
MASTER: I'm not cross with you, little Jacques. You did it for
my sake.
JACQUES: I did. I know the degree to which you love women
with big bottoms.
MASTER: You're good, Jacques. You're a good servant.
Servants should be good and tell their masters what they
want to hear. No useless truths, Jacques.
JACQUES: Fear not, Master. I'm no lover of useless truths. I
don't know anything so stupid as a useless truth.
MASTER: Instance?
JACQUES: Instance: that we are mortal. Or indeed, that this
world is rotten. As if we didn't know. You know the type,
those heroes who come on stage and cry 'This world is
rotten!' The public loves it, but not Jacques, because
Jacques knew it two hundred, four hundred, *eight* hundred
years before, and while that lot cries that the world is
rotten, Jacques prefers to busy himself thinking up things
to please his master . . .
MASTER: . . . his rotten master . . .
JACQUES: . . . his rotten master, things like women with big
bums, as preferred by Sir.
MASTER: Only I and He who looks down on all of us know that
you are the best servant of all servants who ever served.
JACQUES: So: don't ask questions, don't try and find out the
truth, and listen to me: she had a big bottom . . . now:
which one am I talking about?
MASTER: About the shack woman who looked after you.
JACQUES: Yes, I spent a week in bed, during which the doctors
drank all their wine, to such an extent that my benefactors
were looking for a way of getting rid of me as soon as
possible. Happily, one of the doctors looking after me was a
quack up at the château, and his wife intervened on my
behalf and they took me up there with them.

MASTER: So nothing happened between you and the pretty little shack woman?

JACQUES: No.

MASTER: Pity. Oh well. And the doctor's wife, the one who intervened on your behalf, what was she like?

JACQUES: Blonde.

MASTER: Like Agathe.

JACQUES: Long legs.

MASTER: Like Agathe. And behind?

JACQUES: Like so. (*Demonstrates*)

MASTER: Pure Agathe. (*Indignantly*) Oh, the wicked girl. I would've been even harder on her than the Marquis des Arcis was on his little swindler. Harder even than young Bigre on Justine.
(SAINT-OUEN *has been onstage, on the rostrum, for some while, and he listens to the conversation of* JACQUES *and his* MASTER *with some interest.*)

SAINT-OUEN: And why weren't you?

JACQUES: (*To the* MASTER) You hear? He's sending you up! He's a sod, that one, and I told you the first time you told me about him . . .

MASTER: I admit he's a sod, but at this precise moment all he's done is what you did to your friend Bigre.

JACQUES: None the less, it's obvious that he's a sod and I'm not.

MASTER: (*Struck by the truth of this last remark*) You're right. You have both seduced the women of your best friends. None the less, he's a sod and you're not. How do you account for that?

JACQUES: No idea. But I'd say that in this riddle lies a deep truth.

MASTER: It does, and I know which one. The thing that sets you apart is not your actions, but your souls. After you'd cuckolded your friend Bigre, you were drunk with grief, weren't you?

JACQUES: I don't want to dispel your illusions. It wasn't grief that made me drunk, it was joy.

MASTER: You weren't drunk from grief?

JACQUES: It's lousy, but it's true.

MASTER: Jacques, do something for me, would you?

JACQUES: For you? Anything you ask.

MASTER: Let's agree that you were drunk from grief.

JACQUES: If you wish, sir.

MASTER: I wish.

JACQUES: Fine, sir: I was drunk from grief.

MASTER: Thank you. I wish to distinguish you in every possible
way from that sod, (*At these words, he turns and looks at*
SAINT-OUEN *who is still on the rostrum.*) who is, moreover,
not content with having cuckolded me . . .
(MASTER *climbs on to the rostrum.*)

SCENE TWO

SAINT-OUEN: My friend! We must think of revenge now. That
wretched little girl has tricked us both and we must avenge
ourselves together.

JACQUES: Yes, I remember, that's where we stopped before.
Well, Master. What did you say to the rat?

MASTER: (*Turning to* JACQUES *from the rostrum, in a pitiful and
pathetic voice*) Me? Look on me, little Jacques, and weep for
my fate. (*To* SAINT-OUEN) Listen, Saint-Ouen, I'm happy
to forget your betrayal on one condition.

JACQUES: Bravo! don't let him get away with it, Master.

SAINT-OUEN: Anything. I'll do anything. Want me to jump out
of the window? (MASTER *smiles and says nothing.*) Hang
myself? (MASTER *says nothing.*) Drown myself? (MASTER *is
silent.*) Plunge this knife into my breast? Yes, yes! (*Opens
his shirt and holds the knife at his breast.*)

MASTER: Put it away. (*Takes the knife from his hand.*) Now, let's
have a drink, and then I'll tell you the dreadful condition

upon which I'll forgive you . . . Agathe is so very voluptuous!

SAINT-OUEN: If only you knew her as I do!

JACQUES: (*To* SAINT-OUEN) She got long legs?

SAINT-OUEN: (*To* JACQUES, *whispering*) Not really.

JACQUES: And a lovely big bum?

SAINT-OUEN: (*As before*) Tiny.

JACQUES: I see you're a dreamer, Master, which only makes me love you the more.

MASTER: (*To* SAINT-OUEN) I shall tell you my condition. We're going to empty this bottle, and then you're going to tell me all about Agathe. You're going to tell me what she's like in bed. What she says, how she moves. What she does. Her sighs. You'll talk, we'll drink, and I'll imagine . . .

(SAINT-OUEN *says nothing and looks at Jacques's* MASTER.)

MASTER: Well? You agree? What's the problem? Talk! (SAINT-OUEN *says nothing.*) You do understand me?

SAINT-OUEN: Yes.

MASTER: You go along with it?

SAINT-OUEN: Yes.

MASTER: Why aren't you drinking then?

SAINT-OUEN: I'm looking at you.

MASTER: So I see.

SAINT-OUEN: We're the same height. In the dark, we could be taken for each other.

MASTER: What's on your mind? Why haven't you started? I've got a very vivid imagination, you know. For Christ's sake, Saint-Ouen, I can't put up with this much longer. I want you to *talk*. About *her*.

SAINT-OUEN: You're asking me, my friend, to describe one of my nights with Agathe?

MASTER: You don't know the meaning of the word passion! Yes, that's what I'm asking. Is it too much?

SAINT-OUEN: On the contrary. It's very little. But what would you say, if, instead of telling you about a night, I *got* you a night?

MASTER: A night? A real night?

SAINT-OUEN: (*Taking two keys out of his pocket*) The little one is the street key, the other opens the door to Agathe's room. This is what I've done for the past six months: I walk in the street till a pot of basil appears at the window. I open the front door. I close it silently. Silently, I climb the stairs. Silently I open Agathe's door. Next to her room is a wardrobe. I take my clothes off in it. Agathe leaves her door ajar, and, in the dark, she awaits me.

MASTER: And you'll let me take your place.

SAINT-OUEN: With all my heart. I have just one tiny request...

MASTER: What is it? What is it?

SAINT-OUEN: I can say what it is?

MASTER: Of course. Your pleasure is my only desire.

SAINT-OUEN: You are the best friend in the world.

MASTER: Hardly better than you. Now: what can I do for you?

SAINT-OUEN: Stay in her arms till morning. Then I'll show up as if nothing had happened and surprise you.

MASTER: (*With a little shocked laugh*) Oh what a wonderful idea! Isn't it a little cruel, though?

SAINT-OUEN: Not so much cruel – as ... pleasing. Beforehand, I will have taken my clothes off in the wardrobe and when I surprise you, I shall be...

MASTER: What, naked? God, you dirty beast! But will it work? We've only got one set of keys...

SAINT-OUEN: We'll go into the house together. We'll undress together in the wardrobe, and *you'll* get into bed with her. Then when you're ready, you'll give me a sign and I'll simply join you.

MASTER: This is the most wonderful idea!

SAINT-OUEN: Heaven, isn't it? You're on?

MASTER: *Absolutely*! Only...

SAINT-OUEN: Only...?

MASTER: Only ... you know ... no, absolutely! I'm on! It's just – you know, the first time, I'd rather be alone ... later, perhaps, we could ...

SAINT-OUEN: Ah, I see you want to revenge us more than once.

MASTER: It's such a delectable revenge . . .

SAINT-OUEN: You bet. (*He points to the back of the stage, where* AGATHE *is stretched on a step. The* MASTER *advances towards her as if bewitched and* AGATHE *stretches out her arm to him . . .*) Quiet, softly, the whole house is sleeping. (*The* MASTER *stretches out alongside* AGATHE *and takes her in his arms.*)

JACQUES: I congratulate you, Master, but I'm worried for you.

SAINT-OUEN: (*From the rostrum, to* JACQUES) My friend, according to all the rules, a valet should be delighted at the sight of his master being made a fool of.

JACQUES: My Master is a good chap and he obeys me. I don't like other masters, who are not good chaps, leading him by the nose.

SAINT-OUEN: Your master is a cretin and deserves the fate of cretins.

JACQUES: In certain respects, my master is perhaps a halfwit. But I have found in his stupidity a rather likeable wisdom that I seek in vain in your bright little brain.

SAINT-OUEN: Fancy! A servant in love with his master! Observe closely how this escapade turns out for him.

JACQUES: Just at the moment, he's happy, and I'm delighted for him.

SAINT-OUEN: Give it a minute.

JACQUES: For the time being he's happy, and that's enough. What more can we ask than to be happy for the time being?

SAINT-OUEN: It'll cost him, his moment of happiness!

JACQUES: What if in this moment he experiences so much happiness that all the miseries you've got lined up for him add up to nothing by comparison?

SAINT-OUEN: If I thought that I was procuring more happiness than pain for that halfwit, I'd stick this knife in my breast for real.
(*Starts shouting into the wings.*)
Hey, everybody! What're you waiting for? It's nearly day!

SCENE THREE

Uproar and noise. People rush toward the step where Jacques's MASTER *and* AGATHE *are still intertwined; among the crowd,* AGATHE'S MOTHER *and* FATHER *in night clothes, and a* POLICE CONSTABLE.

CONSTABLE: Ladies and gentlemen, silence, please, the *delicto* is distinctly *flagrante*! Monsieur has been caught in the act. As far as I am aware, he is a member of the upper classes, and an honest man. I trust he will make amends for his offence off his own bat and without the intervention of the law.

JACQUES: My God, Master, they've got you.

AGATHE'S FATHER: (*Forcibly restraining his wife from striking their daughter*) Leave her, mother. Things will work themselves out for the best . . .

AGATHE'S MOTHER: (*To Jacques's* MASTER) You've got such an honest look about you, who would've thought you capable of . . .

CONSTABLE: (*To Jacques's* MASTER *who, meanwhile, has got up from the step*) Follow me, please, sir.

MASTER: And where were you thinking of taking me?

CONSTABLE: (*Leading the* MASTER *off*) To prison.

JACQUES: (*Staggered*) Prison?!

MASTER: (*To* JACQUES) Yes, little Jacques, prison . . .
(CONSTABLE *goes off. The little group which had formed around the step disperses. The* MASTER *is alone on the rostrum.* SAINT-OUEN *approaches.*)

SAINT-OUEN: My friend, my friend! This is dreadful. You, in prison! How can it be possible? I've just been at Agathe's; her parents didn't even want to talk; they knew that you're my only friend, they accused me of being responsible for their distress. Agathe didn't tear my eyes out. You understand, I'm sure...

MASTER: But Saint-Ouen, it just needs a word from you to get me off the hook.

SAINT-OUEN: How?

MASTER: How? By telling what happened.

SAINT-OUEN: Yes, I threatened Agathe with that. But I can't. Think what it would look like. Also ... it's your fault.

MASTER: My fault?

SAINT-OUEN: Yes, your fault. If you'd gone along with my little jape, Agathe would have been discovered between two men, and the whole thing would have ended up in derision. But no, you had to be selfish, my friend. You had to take your pleasure alone.

MASTER: Saint-Ouen!

SAINT-OUEN: That's the way it is, chum. You've been punished for your selfishness.

MASTER: (*Reproachfully*) My friend!

(SAINT-OUEN *walks round, then leaves rapidly.*)

JACQUES: (*To his* MASTER) God almighty! When're you going to stop calling him your friend? The whole world can see that he's ensnared you in a trap, you've even denounced him yourself, but still you're blind! And I'm going to be a laughing stock because I've got a halfwit for a master.

SCENE FOUR

The MASTER *turns towards* JACQUES *and during the rest of the dialogue comes down from the rostrum.*

MASTER: If only he were just a halfwit, little Jacques. He's an *unhappy* halfwit, and that's worse. I came out of prison, but not before paying considerable damages for the outrage committed against the young lady's honour . . .

JACQUES: (*Consolingly*) Could've ended up even worse, Master. What if she'd got pregnant!

MASTER: You guessed.

JACQUES: What?

MASTER: Yes.

JACQUES: Not – large with child? (*The* MASTER *nods:* JACQUES *takes him in his arms.*) Master – my poor little master. I do see now that is the worst possible ending a story could have.

(*During this whole scene, the dialogue between* JACQUES *and his* MASTER *is imbued with genuine sadness and is quite without comedy.*)

MASTER: Not only did I have to pay for that little trollop's honour, but I was condemned to undertake the costs of her delivery *and* make provision for the upbringing and education of a brat who bore a quite disgusting resemblance to my friend Saint-Ouen.

JACQUES: Now I see: the worst possible ending a human story can have, is a brat. The sinister full stop to an adventure. The blot at the end of love. And how old would Monsieur your son be now?

MASTER: Ten, any day now. He's been in the country all this time. I'm taking the opportunity on this journey of ours to stop at the house of the people who've been looking after him to pay them off and fix the snotty-nosed little pipsqueak an apprenticeship somewhere.

JACQUES: You remember that at the beginning that lot (*Gesturing to the audience*) asked where we were going, and I replied: who knows where he's going? – Well, you knew all too well where we were going, my sad little master.

MASTER: I want to make a watchmaker out of him. Or a carpenter. A carpenter for preference. He'll turn out endless chair rungs, and he'll produce children who will turn out more chair-rungs, and more children, and those children will in turn turn out innumerable more chairs and innumerable more children . . .

JACQUES: So the world will be crammed with chairs and children. That'll be your revenge.

MASTER: (*With bitter disgust*) Grass will no longer grow. Flowers will stop flowering, and everywhere there will be only chairs and children.

JACQUES: Chairs and children, nothing but chairs and children. What a frightening vision of the future. We're lucky, Master. We're dying in time.

MASTER: (*Thoughtfully*) I do hope so, Jacques, because sometimes I fill with anguish at the idea of this unending repetition of children, of chairs, and of everything . . . You know, yesterday evening, listening to the story of Mme de La Pommeraye, I said to myself: isn't it always the same story which never changes? Because in the end, Mme de La Pommeraye is just a replica of Saint-Ouen. And I'm only another version of your poor friend Bigre and Bigre is nothing but the image of that dupe of a Marquis. And I see no difference between Justine and Agathe and Agathe is a double of that little tramp the Marquis finally felt himself forced to marry.

JACQUES: (*Thoughtfully*) Yes sir, it's like a merry-go-round. You know, my grandpa, the one who put a gag round my mouth, used to read the Bible every night, but it didn't always please him, he used to say that even the Bible endlessly repeated itself, and repetition takes its listeners for imbeciles. And you know what I've been wondering, sir, Whether the one who does all the writing up there hasn't repeated himself an incredible amount and whether he, too, doesn't take us for imbeciles . . . (JACQUES *falls silent and the* MASTER, *sad, makes no reply; a silence, then* JACQUES *makes himself comfort his* MASTER *again.*) Lord above, Master! Don't be sad, I'll do anything to cheer you up: tell you what, Master: I'll tell you how I fell in love.

MASTER: (*Melancholy*) Tell me, Jacques.

JACQUES: When I lost my cherry, I got arseholed.

MASTER: Yes, I know that already.

JACQUES: Oh, don't be cross. I'm going straight on to the surgeon's wife.

MASTER: Is she the one you fell in love with?

JACQUES: No.

MASTER: (*Looking round him with sudden suspicion*) Spare me then and get to the point.

JACQUES: What's the hurry, Master?

MASTER: Something tells me, Jacques, that we haven't got much time left.

JACQUES: You're frightening me, Master.

MASTER: Something tells me you should get on with finishing your story.

JACQUES: Right. I'd been at the surgeon's for a week when I finally was able to get up for the first time.
(*JACQUES is involved in his speech and looks at the audience rather than at his MASTER who is becoming more and more interested in the scenery.*)

JACQUES: It was a lovely day, and I drank even more . . .

MASTER: I think we're just coming to the village where my bastard lives, Jacques.

JACQUES: Sir! You're interrupting at the most beautiful moment. I was still limping badly, I was getting even weaker at the knees, but – it was a lovely day, I can see it as if it was now.
(*Downstage,* SAINT-OUEN *suddenly appears. He doesn't see the* MASTER. *But the* MASTER *sees and watches him.* JACQUES *is facing the audience and is totally absorbed in his speech.*)
It was autumn, sir, the trees were multi-coloured, the sky was blue, and I went down a forest lane, when I saw this girl who was coming towards me to meet me, and I know you're not going to interrupt me, so, it was a lovely day, and this girl came towards me, *please* don't interrupt me, sir, she was just about to meet me, slowly, you know, and she was looking at me, and I was looking at her, and she had this beautiful, sad face, sir, her face was sad, and so beautiful . . .

SAINT-OUEN: (*Finally spots the* MASTER, *and jumps in the air*)
You! My friend . . .
(*The* MASTER *draws his sword:* SAINT-OUEN *does the same.*)
MASTER: Yes, me. Your friend, the best friend you ever had.
(*Throws himself at him; the two men fight*) What are you
doing here? Come to see your son, have you? See if he's fat
enough? Find out if I've plumped him up properly?
JACQUES: (*Watches the fight with dread*) Watch out, sir, take
care!
(*The duel doesn't last long and* SAINT-OUEN *lurches back,
wounded.* JACQUES *bends over him.*)
I think he's had it. Sir: I think this should never have
happened.
(JACQUES *bends over* SAINT-OUEN's *corpse while peasants
rush on stage.*)
MASTER: Jacques, quick, run!
(*He leaves the stage running.*)

SCENE FIVE

JACQUES *has not succeeded in fleeing. Several peasants have laid
hands on him and are holding him with his hands behind his back.*
JACQUES, *his hands bound, is at the back of the stage. The*
CONSTABLE *looks him up and down with contempt.*

CONSTABLE: Well, chum, whatchew got to say about all this,
eh? You're going to be thrown into prison, tried and
hanged.
JACQUES: (*Standing up, at the back of the stage, with his hands
tied behind his back*) I can only tell you what my old captain
always used to say: everything that happens down here is
written up there.

CONSTABLE: A great truth, that.

(He leaves slowly with the other peasants and JACQUES *remains alone on stage throughout the ensuing speech.)*

JACQUES: One can obviously ask the price of what is written up there. Ah master! You think there's any wisdom in my ending my days hanged because you were in love with Agathe? And you'll never find out how I fell in love. That sad beautiful girl was a maid at the château, and I'd been hired at the château as a servant, but you'll never know the end of the story, because they're going to hang me, she was called Denise and I loved her a lot, I never loved anyone again after her, but we only knew each other for a fortnight, will you just think of that, sir, only a fortnight, a fortnight because my then master, who was also Denise's master, gave me to the Comte de Boulay, who then gave me to his elder brother the Captain, who gave me to his nephew, the advocate general of Toulouse, who then gave me to the Comte de Trouville, then the Comte de Trouville gave me to the Marquise de Bellow, who escaped from London with an Englishman, and a nice little scandal that was too, but before fleeing she took the time to recommend me to Captain de Marty, yes, sir, the very one who used to say that everything was written up there, and Captain de Marty gave me to M. Herissant who got me into Mlle Isselin's that you were keeping but who drove you mad because she was thin and hysterical and while she was driving you mad I used to take your mind off it with my old chat and you got fond of me and you would have fed me in my old age, because you promised you would and I know you would have kept your word, we would never have left each other, we were made for each other. Jacques for his Master, his Master for Jacques. And now look at us, apart because of a stupid thing like this. Good God, what's it got to do with me that you let yourself be made an arse of by that rat? Why do I have to be hanged because you've got a good heart and rotten taste? The rubbish that's written up there! Oh, sir, the guy who wrote our story up there must be a really bad poet, the worst bad poet ever, the king, the emperor of bad poets!

YOUNG BIGRE: (*Has appeared at the back of the stage during* JACQUES's *last words: he looks at him questioningly, then calls him*) Jacques!

JACQUES: (*Not looking at him*) Fuck off.

YOUNG BIGRE: That you, Jacques?

JACQUES: Fuck off, the lot of you. I'm talking to my master.

YOUNG BIGRE: Jesus, Jacques, don't you recognize me, then?
(*He grabs* JACQUES *and turns him round.*)

JACQUES: Bigre . . .

YOUNG BIGRE: What they tied your hands up for?

JACQUES: They're going to hang me.

YOUNG BIGRE: Hang you? No . . . my friend. I'm glad to say there are still a few friends around who remember their friends. (*He unties the strings binding* JACQUES's *hands, then turns him round and takes him in his arms.* JACQUES, *in* BIGRE's *arms, laughs deeply.*) What are you laughing for?

JACQUES: I've just been badmouthing a bad poet for being such a bad poet, and now he rushes you along to put his bad poem right and, Bigre, I tell you: even the worst poet in the world couldn't have made up a happier ending to his bad poem.

YOUNG BIGRE: I dunno what you're going on about, but it don't matter. I've never forgotten you, you know. Remember that granary? (*Now he laughs and slaps* JACQUES's *back;* JACQUES *laughs too.*) See it? (*Points to the steps, at the back of the stage*) That's not a granary, my old mate. It's a bloody chapel. It's a temple to faithful friendship. Jacques, you can't begin to guess the happiness you brought us. You signed up for the army, I remember, and one month later, I learned that Justine . . .
(*He pauses meaningfully.*)

JACQUES: Justine. Justine what?

YOUNG BIGRE: Justine (*Another meaningful pause*) was going to have (*Silence*) Go on! Guess! . . . a kid!

JACQUES: You realized one month after I signed up?

YOUNG BIGRE: My dad couldn't say another word after that. He *had* to agree to my marrying Justine and eight months later . . . (*Eloquent pause.*)
JACQUES: What was it?
YOUNG BIGRE: A boy.
JACQUES: He all right, is he?
YOUNG BIGRE: (*Proudly*) What! We called him Jacques in your honour. You'll never believe it, but he even looks a bit like you. You've gotta come and see him. Justine'll be delirious.
JACQUES: (*Turning back*) Dear little master: our stories are comically similar . . .
(YOUNG BIGRE *leads* JACQUES *gaily off; they leave.*)

SCENE SIX

MASTER: (*Comes on to the empty stage. He looks unhappy.*) Jacques! Little Jacquot! (*Looks around him*) Since I lost you, the stage is deserted, like the world, and the world is deserted like an empty stage . . . what wouldn't I give to have you tell me the story of the Sheath and the Cutlass again. It's a disgusting story. That's why I used to deny it, reject it, declare it null and void: so that you could tell it again, and tell each time as if it were the first time . . . Ah, little Jacques! if only I could also repudiate the story of Saint-Ouen . . . But only your lovely stories can be repudiated and there's no going back on my stupid escapade and I'm well and truly in it up to the neck and I'm in it without you and without those wonderful bums that you could summon up with a single light movement of those eloquent lips of yours . . . (*He starts reciting in a dreamy voice as if he were speaking blank verse.*) Those buttocks round and curvéd like the moon! . . . (*Normal voice*) But you were right. We don't know where we're

83

going. I thought I was going to visit my little bastard and I
went and lost my dear little Jacques for ever and ever.

JACQUES: (*Coming towards him from the other side of the stage*)
Little master!

MASTER: (*Turning round, astonished*) Jacques!

JACQUES: Well, you know what the Innkeeper said, that
splendid woman with her imposing rear: we can't live
without each other. (MASTER *is gripped with powerful
emotion*: JACQUES *comforts him in his arms*.) There, there,
come on, tell me where we're going.

MASTER: Does anyone know where they're going?

JACQUES: Not a person in the world.

MASTER: Not one.

JACQUES: Well then, lead me.

MASTER: How can I lead you when we don't know where we're
going?

JACQUES: As written up there. You're my master and it's your
mission in life to lead me.

MASTER: Ah yes, but you've forgotten what's written a little
further on. It is indeed the master who gives the orders, but
it's Jacques who chooses which ones. I'm waiting.

JACQUES: Right. I want you to lead me . . . forwards.

MASTER: (*Looking around, rather embarrassed*) I'd love to, but –
where is forward?

JACQUES: I'll tell you a great secret. One of mankind's oldest
insights. Forward is anywhere.

MASTER: (*Looking around him in a wide arc*) Anywhere?

JACQUES: (*Describing a circle with a broad gesture of his arm*) No
matter where you look, anywhere is forward.

MASTER: (*Without enthusiasm*) Oh that's magnificent, Jacques!
Magnificent!
(*He slowly turns round.*)

JACQUES: (*With melancholy*) Yes sir, I find it rather marvellous,
too.

MASTER: (*After a brief bit of business, sadly*) Well then, Jacques:
forward!
(*They slant themselves towards the back of the stage.*)